And no, I'm not going to fall in love with him.

Not on your life.

—

Juicy Pickle is the wildest not-love story that ever became a love story between a boss and his former assistant, stuck together on a private island with a manual-crank margarita machine and a ten-gallon bucket of pickles, surviving primarily on adrenaline and stress-banging.

Edition 1.0

Casey Shay Press
PO Box 160116
Austin, TX 78716
www.jjknight.com

Paperback ISBN: 9781938150319

by JJ Knight
the *USA Today* bestselling author of

Big Pickle ~ Hot Pickle ~ Spicy Pickle
Tasty Mango ~ Tasty Pickle
Royal Pickle ~ Royal Rebel ~ Royal Escape
Juicy Pickle
Second Chance Santa
The Wedding Confession
The Wedding Shake-up
Single Dad on Top ~ The Accidental Harem
Uncaged Love ~ Fight for Her ~ Reckless Attraction

Want to make sure you don't miss a release?
Sign up for emails or texts at www.jjknight.com/news

ABOUT JUICY PICKLE

Can you imagine getting stuck alone on a deserted island with the person you hate most in the world? And no end in sight?

Well, that's me. Bailey Johansson, former assistant to the absolute worst boss ever to boss in the boss world. Stranded on a tiny island owned by a cruise line in an abandoned party hut.

In a tropical storm.

This is not a love story.

It's not a tale of redemption or heroism.

It's a revenge drama. No — a revenge COMEDY.

Because I'll get the last laugh. The cruise ship leaving early due to an approaching storm while we yelled at each other on the opposite beach was a SIGN.

I'm going to get that man back for everything he did to me. I've decided that Mr. Juicy, as my old coworkers called him (yeah, THAT'S a story), is going to rue the day he ever fired me.

1

BAILEY

Confidence, Bailey, confidence.

You can fake anything with the right attitude.

Fake competence.

Fake knowledge.

Fake orgasms.

Ha.

I'm good at those. Nobody's ever really hit the *spot*, you know? Close. But no banana.

Banana, ha.

Salami.

Pickle.

I kill myself.

Confidence, I repeat inside my head as I approach the ticket desk. You can pull off the fake of the century. You deserve this. You earned it before it was mercilessly snatched from you.

"Hello!" says a chirpy voice. The woman at the desk is cute and perky in her snazzy Blue Sapphire uniform.

"You must be here for the Dougherty Inc. employee cruise."

Time to shine.

I lean my arm on the counter to show how casual I feel. How much I *belong*. "I most definitely am. I've worked for Dougherty for two years."

Minus the last two weeks, since getting fired by my horrible boss, Rhett Armstrong. But she can't know that. And I still have my cruise pass on my phone.

"Lovely." She rests her hands on the keyboard. "First and last name?"

"Bailey Johansson."

"Like Scarlett Johansson?"

"No relation."

The woman's coral-colored lips smile adoringly. "Of course."

My hairline pops with sweat. I've come early, really early, twenty minutes before the official start of the check-in time, hoping to get on the boat, in my room, and in hiding until we're in the middle of the ocean. Then nobody can kick me off, not even the evil Rhett Armstrong.

I will get my Bahamas cruise, despite getting axed.

I earned this vacation, damn it. I worked my butt off, making sure I pleased my tyrant of a boss so that nothing would get in the way of me and this anniversary cruise for the company.

I endured Rhett. His rages. His perfectionism. His ridiculous hours.

I shoved my feelings into my shoes to avoid anything coming between me and my white sandy beaches.

I did not make it.

But I was very close, close enough to have gotten a boarding pass before my untimely termination. So, I'm here anyway.

The woman taps on the keys, a frown on her face. "I'm not seeing your cabin assignment."

I'm ready for this.

"I only just confirmed that I could come. I might not have been assigned with the others." I turn my phone to her to show her the pass that was sent to me a month ago, before the disaster.

She peers at it and keeps tapping.

"My sister was pregnant and due this week. I wanted to be there for her. But the baby came early, so I'm here!" This is all a total lie. I'm an only child.

"That's lovely." She moves her mouse around. "Okay, I see you on the original passenger list. I'm so glad you could make it. Did she have a boy or a girl?"

"A boy. Maxwell." Maxwell is the name of my cat. I love him like I would a nephew. If I had one. Or a sister.

"How precious. I got you assigned a cabin."

"Oh, good. Thank you so much." First hurdle crossed.

She swipes a keycard and prints several tags for my luggage. "You can wait in Lounge A. Your bags will be waiting in your cabin." She passes me the card.

"Oh, I can't get on board?" I hear voices behind me. Someone else is early. I press my floppy sun hat lower on my head and resist the urge to put on the sunglasses tucked into the square neckline of my sundress.

"We will board you all together. The lounge has a

breakfast buffet and a coffee bar all ready for you. Enjoy talking to your co-workers as you wait."

She looks behind me to greet the approaching guests.

Oh, boy. I didn't bank on having to stand around before we got on the yacht.

I beeline for the open double doors of Lounge A, then hesitate before entering, making sure no one is there. Only a woman in a chef hat and blue uniform is inside, stacking plates on a long table.

I move beyond the doors, stepping to one side before turning to peer out at the group behind me. I recognize Matthew from accounting. He was the one who handled my boss's expense checks. The woman with him is probably his wife.

Another couple enters the lobby, Gina from HR and her husband. I definitely can't let her see me. She did my exit interview, where I dropped more F-bombs than a pissed-off truck driver. I take a step back from the door. This is going to be trickier than I thought.

I survey the lounge. There's a coffee bar with large brown carafes and perfect rows of gleaming white mugs. A long buffet is lined with silver chafing dishes.

My stomach growls. Too bad, morning belly, we have to hide.

There's a ficus plant in one corner that might offer some protection, but not when the room gets busy. The chef heads through a side door, presumably to a kitchen. I don't know how long I could hang out in there before someone ushered me out.

Otherwise, there's only this door to the front desk.

I peer into the lobby. A second Blue Sapphire employee has arrived to help with check-in, so both Matthew and Gina are occupied with getting their bags tagged.

There's a matching set of doors on the opposite side of the desk, presumably another lounge. But those are shut tight. They might be locked.

Another short hall leads to the bathrooms. Of course. That's a safe place, and I better get there before anyone else arrives.

I pin my straw bag to my side with my elbow and angle my head so that my hat hides my face from my former co-workers. Then I race toward the women's bathroom, push through the door, and quickly lock myself in the last stall.

I guess I'll stay here as long as possible.

The toilet seat is up from being cleaned. I drop it down, perching delicately on the edge. I wish I'd asked how long it would be before we boarded the boat. I can't believe we're going in a group. This isn't how I thought it would go at all!

And now if I get caught, my luggage is already in a cabin. I might never get it back!

I start to stomp my foot, but I slip into the toilet. I catch myself just before my butt hits the water.

"Get it together, Bailey," I tell myself.

Long moments pass. It's warm in the bathroom. Sweat pops on my brow. I pull out my phone, realize the signal in here is terrible, and shove it back in my bag.

Then, the bathroom door opens and I hold my breath, listening. Someone steps in, enters the stall two down from mine, and the sound of pee hitting the water breaks the silence.

I duck down to check out the shoes. I recognize those orthopedics. They belong to Marney in marketing, without a doubt. She hated me, mainly over my never-ending requisitions, as if they were my fault and not Rhett's. She'd rat me out in a heartbeat.

And if I recognize *her* shoes, then she might know mine. I stand on the toilet, kicking myself for not wearing something plain that wouldn't give me away. I love these pink Bernie Mevs, a perfect match for my pink-and-yellow sundress, but they are too obvious and unique.

The toilet flushes, and shortly after, the outer door opens again. Is someone else here?

I wait, straining to listen, then realize the room is silent.

No, Marney from marketing just doesn't wash her hands.

I shift carefully to get down, but I'm not coordinated enough for toilet squatting. I lose my balance, and one of my beautiful Bernie Mevs hits the toilet water with a decisive splash.

"Noooo," I hiss, stepping to the ground and pulling my dripping foot from the bowl. "No, no, no, no."

This is Rhett Armstrong's fault. All of it.

But I'm going to make it onto this boat if it's the last thing I do.

At least the water was clean. I unroll toilet paper, kicking off my shoe to dry my dripping foot. Then I do my best to soak up the wetness from the shoe. The pink is twice as dark as on the dry one. It looks ridiculous.

Damn it all.

How weird would it be to go barefoot? Weirder than shoes of different colors?

I toss the wet paper into the toilet and flush.

Stupid Rhett. Stupid firing. Stupid job.

After what feels like eternity, the door opens again. I decide to hell with it and take off both shoes, setting them on top of the metal box attached to the stall for non-flushable items. The floor was just mopped. My feet will be fine.

I don't have to look under the door to know the person who entered is Viola, my former work bestie. She was directly involved in getting me fired, so obviously, we don't talk anymore.

I mourned the loss of our friendship as much as the job. But I recognize the clop-clop of her Jimmy Choo mules. She wears them everywhere. She never got over finding them for five dollars at Goodwill and tells every stranger she meets all about it, whether they ask or not.

"Did you see Rhett?" Viola asks, and I realize someone else came in with her.

I duck down to look at the other person's shoes. Black flip-flops, totally nondescript. That could be anyone.

Who would Viola come in with? We never ate lunch with anyone else. For Viola, office gossip was a blood sport, and she had no love for anyone but me.

And Rhett, of course, the subject of her never-ending Cinderella fantasy where she bangs him in his imaginary penthouse and they fly off in the private jet that also does not exist. Dougherty isn't that rich of a company, even though this cruise is pretty posh.

Viola works in marketing with Marney. Maybe she's with Kenna from accounting? I peer down again. I can't tell by the ankles, but the legs are wearing capri yoga pants, and that's totally a Kenna outfit.

Viola keeps talking. She's like that. It can be hard to get a word in edge-wise. "See why we call him Mr. Juicy? He looks perfectly delicious in those shorts and that polo. Gawd. I'm going to juice that fruit on this cruise if it's the last thing I do."

"You sure?"

Yep, that's Kenna. Her brown ponytail and make-up-free face come instantly to mind.

I peer through the crack in the door. I can only see Viola. She's peacocking in a blue crop top and bright pink shorts with a silver sparkle belt. Her mixed blonde-and-black hair is twisted into an updo with curls popping out the top. It's adorable.

I want to tell her it's gorgeous, but she's not my bestie anymore. Our falling out is as permanent as the "asshole" she once wrote in Sharpie on a white sofa at a party. The man who lived there pinched her butt in the back hall and called her "fatty." Viola exalts her curves.

She coats her lips with a pink the exact shade of her shorts. "Mark my words. Rhett Armstrong is in the bag."

I can't see Kenna's reaction, but Viola blows a kiss at herself in the mirror. "Let's get out there. They're about to board."

Are they?

I wait until Viola and Kenna have left the bathroom, then I carefully slip my shoes into my straw bag and exit the stall.

I slowly pull the outer door open.

I can only see the lounge door and a narrow swath of the lobby, but it's bustling. People talk and laugh, holding coffee cups and plates.

My traitorous stomach growls again.

Hush, now.

I spot Rhett and almost stumble backward.

Viola is right. He looks good. He's tall and tan, his dark hair sweeping across his forehead like Henry Cavill's version of Superman. He's always had broad shoulders, but they are particularly prominent in his pale-yellow polo, the fabric stretching over his chest.

He smiles and shakes hands with everyone as if he owns the company. Which he does not. But he's definitely Dougherty's right-hand man.

Dougherty himself never visits the office. I don't know if he's even coming on the cruise. I worked there for two years and never met him, not even at a holiday party.

A woman I don't know heads for the bathroom, so I quickly back away from the door and retreat to my stall.

She pees quickly, washes swiftly, and heads out. While the door is open, I hear an announcement. "If you have been checked in, you may proceed out the side door to the dock."

I might have to wait to be the very last person on. Riskier than my dashed plan of being first, but doable.

I peer out the door again. It looks like most of the company has checked in while I hid. They're all inching in the same direction.

Rhett moves out of view. Then Viola and Kenna. Marney. The accounting crew. A couple of guys from tech. Husbands and wives, girlfriends, boyfriends.

When no one is visible, I step out and creep to the end of the hall. The early group is already disappearing through a glass door out the back of the lobby.

There are several people checking in, but I only know Peter from the maintenance staff and he probably won't notice me. He's staring at his phone.

I'll take advantage of the lull.

I swiftly cross the lobby to the side door, where a woman smiles at me. "You have your keycard?"

I nod.

She notices my bare feet but says nothing.

Outside, a sidewalk lined with decorative ropes leads to the dock. Men and women in blue suits with white caps gesture to us to keep moving. I walk slowly, trying to avoid catching up with the rest of the group. The gap between them and me stretches out.

I've got this.

When I arrive at the metal ramp, a man holds out his hand to help me across the tiny gap between the dock and the threshold to the ship. "Watch your step."

I hold his warm hand for only a moment, then I'm on the boat!

Inside the entrance, a woman waits, alone in a wood-paneled entryway. "Let me check your card, and I'll direct you to your cabin."

I pull it from the front pocket of my bag. She taps in the number, and a diagram appears on the screen. "Here's where we are," she says, pointing to a pulsing green dot. Dotted lines appear. "Follow the hallway to the right until it ends, then go up one set of stairs and your cabin will be about five doors down."

I take my card. "Thank you."

Voices trickle in from the outdoors. People are coming. I hurry toward the stairs, my feet flying along the navy carpet patterned with silver diamonds.

The boat smells lightly of cleaners and the sharp tang of the ocean. The walls are pale blue fading into white near the top, crystals affixed to the wallpaper in an artsy scatter, glinting in the wall lamps. It's fancy.

The upstairs hall is mercifully empty. I find my door, scan my card, then I'm in my room.

Safe.

I let out a long sigh and look around.

The cabin is larger than I expected for a cruise. A narrow bed fills one side with a sofa on the other. A gold-framed instructional image explains how to pull out the sofa to make an extra-large bed that spans the cabin. Cool.

The bathroom is blue and silver with a shower, sink, and toilet. A sliding door on the other side leads to a balcony so tiny that only one person can fit. But it's there.

My cabin is ocean-side, and the bright blue water fills the horizon.

I've done it.

A knock at the door startles me so hard that I whip

around and bang my knee on the corner of the bed. Damn it! I half-hop, half-stumble to the peephole. *Please don't be Rhett Armstrong.*

A young man in a blue uniform stands outside with my mismatched bags. Thank God. I twist the lock and open the door.

"So sorry for the delay, ma'am. Here are your bags." He rolls them inside. "Sorry if I'm in a hurry. We're a little behind." He tips his hat and heads back out.

I press my hand to my chest to slow my slamming heart. You're okay, Bailey. Just hole up until we're away from the dock.

I start to close the door.

A shadow is my first hint someone is coming.

Please be another employee!

But I see a classic boat shoe, an ankle, and a well-toned leg.

It's Rhett.

Oh, God.

I slam the door right as I spot his yellow shirt and sweeping hair.

Did he see me?

I lean against the door and close my eyes, waiting for the worst.

2

———

RHETT

Who did I just see?

I hesitate outside the door as it slams shut. It couldn't be.

I fired Bailey Johansson two weeks ago. Good timing, too, as I couldn't have her on this cruise. She was always the forbidden fruit I found hard to resist.

I consider knocking on the door, then realize I would look really foolish if it was some brown-haired girlfriend of an employee. Or worse, a member of Dougherty Inc. I ought to have recognized.

I shake my head. Figures even the ghost of Bailey would haunt me on this trip. I'll probably see her every time I turn a corner. I refuse to feel guilty about what happened to her job in the end. There was no recovering from what she did to the company.

Bright voices come up from behind. I glance over my shoulder and spot Viola Jennings and a young woman I'm not wholly familiar with. They're coming down the corridor, heading right for me.

"Oh, Rhett! Are we on the same hall?" Viola's voice is a sing-song.

I want to hurry away, but that's not how it works when the buck stops with you. I pause and give the women a pinched smile.

"I'm actually one deck up," I tell Viola. She looks like a poppy in all her bright colors. And she's Bailey's best friend. I saw them having lunch in the courtyard almost every day. Anything I say to this woman will get back to my former assistant, if not now, then when we return.

"Of course you are," Viola says, her gold earrings swinging. "I do hope you'll give me a tour. I'd love to see how the other half lives on a cruise ship."

"All the cabins on Blue Sapphire Cruises are well appointed," I say. "I hope you have a wonderful time. Please excuse me."

And I'm off, striding as quickly as possible to the stairwell that leads to the executive suites.

Viola. Bailey. Two peas in a pod.

I haven't had time to replace Bailey since I abruptly let her go. I had a lot of loose ends to tie up before getting on this boat for four days, potentially completely unavailable for our clients.

If anyone asked me, I would have cautioned against bringing the entire company on a boat with only temp employees manning the office phones. If the satellite service doesn't function correctly once we're out at sea, any emergencies will go unattended.

But it wasn't my call in the end. I got the memo to celebrate the anniversary in style, and this is certainly it.

I signed off on the budget that was given to me. We could have hired several new employees for the cost of it.

For what? A few days of getting drunk and sunburned, and acting inappropriately with coworkers?

I'll be in my room as much as humanly possible.

Hopefully, with a working satellite feed.

I pass a dozen other employees as I make my way to my suite. Unlike the high-end hotels, there aren't secure floors on Blue Sapphire Cruises. Their policy is to secure the whole ship, not any particular part of it. These cruises are normally the playground of celebrities, billionaires, and royalty.

But here we are.

The upper deck suites don't have keycards, but are programmed with a thumbprint. I press my finger to the pad and the lock pops open. The woman at check-in informed me that I could authorize up to ten additional thumbprints to enter my suite and remove them just as easily. She seemed to think I might make use of it.

I can't imagine churning through that many hookups in four days. Okay, maybe. But not on a work trip.

And I'm not one to fraternize with employees. She definitely pegged me wrong on that score.

The room smells of ocean air, the artificial kind. Even so, it's a nice touch.

The decor is silver and blue, tailored with little frill. I like it. My suitcase is loaded onto a rack, and my laptop bag rests on a gleaming cherrywood desk with a plush office chair. A large monitor is prepped and ready to be a second screen. I'm clearly not the only executive to ever work on a cruise. This will do nicely.

I've only gotten as far as setting my laptop on the desk and extracting the charging cord when someone knocks on the door.

"Rhett?"

It's Gloria from HR. She's functioning as my temporary assistant until she gets me a slate of new ones to choose from, hopefully shortly after this trip.

I open the door. She's standing there looking extremely incongruous in a red one-piece swimsuit with a built-in skirt, palm tree flip-flops, and an armful of official-looking leather-bound binders.

"I was worried that the signal wouldn't be strong, so I had Monica print last month's dailies for you to look over. I figured you'd be working." She glances meaningfully behind me at my open laptop.

Maybe I should hire Gloria. But no, she's top-notch in HR. She'll find me someone.

I take the binders. "That was very resourceful of you. Thank you."

"Do try to enjoy yourself." She passes me a single sheet of paper. "This is the itinerary for the weekend. I highlighted the events where your absence might be noticed. So you can prioritize."

Gloria gets me.

I manage a genuine smile for her. "Thank you."

She grins back, turning her wedding band on her finger as if my smile means she should consider taking it off. I'm aware that quite a few employees have expressed their determination to get me to break my fraternizing rule. Surely she isn't one of them.

"I have to find Frank." Her voice is a rush. "My husband. Of twenty-four years."

I bite back another smile as she backs up, almost tripping on the carpet.

"Thank you for these, Gloria." I hold up the binders. Then I shut the door.

I don't get it. I behave like a roaring curmudgeon at work in order to keep a suitable distance between me and the female employees, but I swear it has the opposite effect.

It's taxing, reining myself in like I do. I'm a ridiculous flirt in the off hours. It's essential, however, that I keep my dating life completely separate from work.

And preferably private. I wouldn't like any exploits getting back to Dougherty Inc. Thankfully, I'm not prominent enough to ever make gossip columns, not like my brother Axel. After the half-billion-dollar sale of a hiking app, he became notorious and couldn't sneeze on a woman without some rag writing a story about it.

Axel lets me know when there are big events at the castle near him, and often my other brother Court and I will fly there and cut loose while far from our home bases.

Maybe I'm due for one of those jaunts.

But first, to get through this one.

I review the itinerary. We set sail shortly with a bon voyage champagne toast, which isn't highlighted. Then there is mustering, which is a mandatory safety lesson involving the lifeboats.

Then there's a poolside welcome party, which is highlighted. Gloria has written "Speech!" in the margin.

Sometimes I think it's unfortunate that the Dougherty of Dougherty Inc. isn't an actual person. But if Uncle Sherman wants this company to function outside of the Pickle enterprises, I have to honor his wishes and keep him out of it.

And that means a poolside speech.

I plunk down into the chair. The days are planned within an inch of their lives. Karaoke, thankfully not highlighted. Sunset serenade with a live band. A midnight buffet. Then tomorrow we reach a small private island owned by Blue Sapphire. Pristine beaches and solitude from the entire world.

Highlighted.

Damn.

I set the list aside and boot up my machine. I only have half an hour until mustering, and I'd like to make a dent in these figures before I'm interrupted by my duties.

And then what ought to be a party, but cannot and will not be one for me, will commence.

And mercifully, none of the activities I will endure this weekend will involve my former assistant, Bailey Johansson.

3

———

BAILEY

I sit on the bed, awaiting my fate.

But then I hear Viola. She's talking in the flirting register, a full half-octave higher than normal. The gossip tone, for reference, is lower than usual.

She and Rhett have a conversation right outside my door. Sweat sprouts along my hairline. Will he mention me? Ask her if I'm here somehow?

But he only explains he's on another floor and excuses himself.

I let out a long breath.

Viola sounds put out when she says, "He didn't even notice my outfit!"

Kenna is with her. "He never compliments anyone's outfits."

"He didn't even look me over!"

I can picture her expression, her body posture. She'll have her arms crossed over her chest in such a way that pushes her boobs up. Her carefully stenciled eyebrows will aim for the bridge of her nose.

I know all of her pouts, every disdainful look. We spent most of our waking hours together, driving to work in my car, visiting the coffee cart for matching caramel lattes, eating lunch in the courtyard, and often hanging out in her cube or at my desk outside Rhett's office.

We did countless happy hours and too many weekend drinking binges to count. She wasn't an easy best friend, a little self-centered, a bit demanding, but she was loyal. She liked to say, "Bailey, it's you and me against the world of Dougherty Inc."

And then it all fell apart.

"Let's find our rooms!" Viola says. "All is not lost. Not by a long shot. I still have the pink bikini. Nobody denies Viola Jennings in a pink bikini."

Kenna either has no answer to that or says it too softly to hear.

I move my bags away from the door. I haven't thought much past my triumphant stowaway mission.

Now that I'm here, I'm not sure what to do. I have to wait for us to embark, that's for sure. But then, do I simply waltz out and take a dip in the pool? Challenge George in accounting to a game of shuffleboard? Take the lion's share of the prime rib from the lunch buffet?

I do love prime rib.

I suddenly remember that scene from *Titanic* when they accuse Jack of stealing the fancy diamond and handcuff him to a pipe in the belly of the ship. Will they do that to me if I'm discovered? I've mapped our route, and the only place they can put me off is the stopover in Freeport, Bahamas. I'd have to get a ticket home, but maybe I can sleep on the beach, bum drinks off hot tourists, and extend the vacay.

Oh, Rhett Armstrong will be so mad when he realizes what I've done.

He just might kick me off the boat. I picture myself, sunburned and pathetic, floating behind the cruise ship on a raft tied to the back.

I'll have to risk it. I didn't sneak onto this cruise to sit like a frightened mouse in my cabin.

A long, low blow of a horn sounds from the back of the ship. I think that means we're about to leave the dock.

I move to my teeny tiny balcony and pull the curtains close to either side of my face as I peer out. Not that I need to hide. The gray-blue of the ocean spreads across the horizon, only a thin white line separating the water from the sky.

Other cruise boats dot the vastness of the space, all at varying distances from the shore. Some appear to be coming in rather than going out, but it isn't easy to tell.

Something rumbles far below the floor of the cabin. The moderately uneasy feeling that the world isn't standing still becomes a hair stronger. At first, I can't discern if we're moving or not. I stare at a white column in the water farther along the shore to see if it moves, but it's impossible to be sure.

But then we gain steam. A great cheer erupts from somewhere above. The sendoff. I hate to miss it, but it doesn't seem safe to leave my cabin yet.

I open my suitcase and find a pair of flip-flops to

replace my mismatched Bernie Mevs. Those I set out on the small table so the wet one can dry.

If my room faced the other way, I'd know when we're a good distance from the shore, but for now I can only wait. I sit by the slit in the curtains, watching the waves over the water.

An announcement piped into the room startles me.

"All passengers are required to muster on Deck 1 in a half-hour. This is a mandatory safety check. All rooms will be visited to ensure participation."

Oh. I didn't know about this. Surely if we're practicing safety, we're well underway? Is a half-hour out far enough away to not return to shore and eject a stowaway?

I glance around the room. There is literally nowhere to hide when they check the room. There's no way to hide beneath the bed or sofa. I move to the bathroom. The door slides left to right, so there is nothing to stand behind. The shower is clear glass.

Time to get creative.

In the corner, between the bed and the tiny balcony, is a small desk. I pull the chair aside and slide my suitcase next to it. This creates a hidey-hole beneath the desk, obscured by the suitcase.

I could still be spotted through the legs of the chair, however. I unzip my bag and pull out a dark blue maxi dress. I drape it over the chair, letting the long skirt fall to the ground.

There. Now it would take a hard look for someone to notice me.

Twenty minutes until mustering. I don't want to

cram myself under the desk for that long, so I fall back on the bed, staring up at the ceiling. It's fancy, tin squares pressed into ornate designs. I've only seen ceilings like this in pictures from decorator magazines. I have very little opportunity for upscale things in my life.

Truth is, I've been hanging by a thread for a long time. My parents couldn't afford to send me to college, so I cobbled together a few scholarships, several jobs, and a brutal amount of student loans to get my degree in political science.

I had this great dream of interning at the state capitaol, then making my way to the national stage. Maybe I would be a speech writer. Or a strategist. I didn't see myself running for office, not a chance, but being someone's right-hand woman.

I could help make change, first in Florida, then the US of A.

I was so naïve.

My starry-eyed vision held true freshman year, and partway into the second. Then I began to take classes in my major, and the real picture became clear. Rich kids got the good internships, the ones where you worked for free but got access to the top offices. I couldn't take those, as I had too many schedules to juggle. I had to pay my way.

Family friends and their contacts were the primary way to get in. Everyone seemed to know someone. I applied right and left and didn't get a single bite, even though my grades were good. It was my references that weren't right.

Nobody was impressed by a father who works at

Kwik-e-Mart and a mother who does clothing alterations. And even though my bosses were glowing in their letters, it wasn't impressive to have curried favor with the manager at Bucky's Burgers.

In hindsight, I should have gotten to know my professors better. I didn't realize they would be my only hope until I was deep into my junior year and most of the good spots for my class were already allocated.

My poli-sci advisor helped me land a clerking spot, but for the traffic court. That got me nowhere, as everyone in that department had already been passed over for any kind of preferential treatment.

I did, however, meet Melanie Billet, who was the assistant to Rhett Armstrong before me. She had the worst time with parking citations. I got to know her when she broke down crying one day at the ticket office and I sat next to her and held out a tissue.

We got her situation handled before she was issued a warrant for outstanding fines. She came by a week later with chocolate croissants and coffee, and we struck up a friendly acquaintance punctuated by her occasional visits with more tickets, which she kept up with after that.

She told me about Dougherty Inc. and Rhett, and eventually, that she was planning to leave and move to Boston. By then, graduation was looming, and none of my applications were panning out. I asked her if entry-level positions were available at her company, maybe vacated by someone who would move into her position.

She suggested I meet Rhett Armstrong and go for the gold. I had a solid degree, and being an assistant for the head of a company like Dougherty had some prestige. The job was more about understanding what Rhett needed done than anything else.

At no point did she tell me he was a tyrant. In fact, she insisted he was a perfectly reasonable boss.

Only after I was hired did he reveal his true self.

The self that is somewhere on this boat.

I check my phone. Fifteen minutes have passed while I lay staring at the ceiling tin.

The curtains have shifted slightly, revealing unbroken ocean as far as I can see. Surely we are far enough out that I'm safe.

I'm debating the mustering issue again when the quiet is broken with a second announcement.

"All guests aboard the Blue Sapphire should please make their way to Deck 1 for compulsory mustering. Everyone aboard must participate in this safety activity."

I glance at the door. Risk it or hide?

The memory of Rhett's hard features from my last day of work settles it. He fired me with no warning, no notice, no time to say goodbye. Two security guards arrived with boxes for me to pack, and I wasn't even able to log out of my computer.

Gone.

And why? One convincing act by my so-called best friend.

I don't even know why she did it. It's not like Rhett has ever given her the time of day. She didn't have to choose between him and me when she brought him those marketing documents that supposedly proved I was milking the company.

But she did, and here we are.

No, that steely glare and rock-hard jaw aren't something I should forget. If he acted harshly and decisively then, he'll do it again. He'll make them turn this boat around.

I need to hide from him as long as possible.

So, I drop to my knees and crawl into my hiding spot right as someone knocks on my door.

"Mustering!" a voice calls. "Time to go to Deck 1 for instructions!"

I bang my head on the desk as I scramble to pull the chair close. I can't see anything but my suitcase and the cushioned seat.

I'll have to wait like a hermit crab in a hole.

4

———

RHETT

Mustering proved simple. We were arranged by our assigned life boat, shown the location of the jackets, and sent on our way. Within fifteen minutes, I should have been able to head back to my cabin.

But I'm surrounded by various employees, all shaking my hand and thanking me for such an unexpectedly lush experience.

I struggle with who some of them are, and briefly wish for Bailey at my side, whispering each one's name and department. She had the pulse of the company. She knew everyone. She was subtle, so I never stumbled, often feeding me a tidbit about a spouse or a child or a recent trip so that I appeared involved.

Damn it.

Stop thinking of Bailey Johansson.

She was the worst sort of incompetent in the end, a situation I have yet to fully investigate and explain to Uncle Sherman. In fact, the dailies I have in my cabin should sort it all. Half a million wasted on a fraudulent marketing scheme is going to hurt. He won't fire me. He's a big believer in both family and redemption.

But his disappointment will be about as bad.

I can't believe this happened on my watch. I got too reliant on Bailey and her research, her opinions, and her involvement beyond the scope of her duties. She seemed so smart, so competent, so trustworthy.

And…I'm thinking about her again.

She's not bereft. She has a live-in boyfriend named Maxwell who seems to do well. I heard her talking to Viola once about his expensive habits and laughing that it was a good thing they could afford his lavish lifestyle. Apparently he has a Persian bed? Or they do.

I definitely don't need to be thinking about Bailey in bed with this mysterious Maxwell. She never brought him to company parties, but I can imagine him. Swarthy, built, well dressed.

And I'm still thinking about Bailey Johansson.

After this cruise, and after I settle the situation with the marketing fiasco, I'm due a visit to my brothers to cut loose. I have to get that woman out of my head.

"So, do you agree, Mr. Armstrong?" A gray-haired woman seems to expect an answer from me. Who did she say she was?

I can only give her a disarming smile, one I normally reserve for non-work situations. "I find it best if I keep my often controversial positions to myself."

The woman giggles like a teen, her hand on my arm.

I'm stuck.

A man walks up, vaguely familiar as someone from

the mailroom. "Lottie, let's head to the hot tub." He pulls the woman, presumably his wife, away from me. "Nice to see you, Mr. Armstrong." He seems a little put out that she's hanging on me like a groupie. They're both sixty, easy.

But his leaving means I'm momentarily alone. I glance around. No one is waiting to see me. I can make my escape. I take long, decisive strides away from the open deck and toward the main body of the ship.

I've almost made it when Viola turns up again, this time in a pink bikini and white mesh cover-up.

Here we go again.

"Rhett." Her voice is low and throaty. "You're not dressed for a pool party. I hear you're giving the welcome speech." She tugs on the tie to her bikini top as if flirting with the idea of pulling it loose.

This is one I need to avoid. When Bailey was around, Viola wasn't this forward. Or maybe it's the informality of the cruise.

"I am, and you're right." I quickly sidestep around her. "I should go change. Cheers!"

Cheers? Where did that come from?

The woman with Viola hangs back, half in shadow. She watches me with something approaching concern mixed with pity. I guess she's the new workplace wingman for Viola now that Bailey's gone.

I walk swiftly back to my deck, taking the stairs two at a time. It must have been difficult for Viola to bring the marketing issue to my attention, knowing it would look bad for Bailey. But it was Viola's department that was the most affected. When I double checked with

Marney before confronting Bailey, Marney confirmed that the budget had swelled the last quarter, all requests from my office.

And that's on Bailey.

The dailies will tell me more. Every requisition, every payment. I've asked accounting for an audit, but I'd like to review the books myself as well. With my schedule cleared of meetings, this cruise is the perfect time.

I heave a sigh when I'm back in my room, but it's short-lived. Gloria's highlighted reminder warns me about the welcome speech I have to deliver. Only half an hour until that.

Normally Bailey would have written a few words for me, but it's fine that I'm doing it myself. I liked her style, and it was nice to hand that task to someone who did it well, but I don't mind speeches.

I open my bag to extract a pair of swim trunks. I will look the part, even if I don't participate any more than necessary. Viola was right. I need to at least give the appearance of being involved in the fun.

If I had my way, if I could be the person I want to be on this trip and not the boss, I would be the first in the pool, the last to shut down the bar. I'd get incredibly inappropriate with a woman in the hot tub and locate a spot to get sunburned in all the wrong places with someone and lick sweat from her nipples.

Nobody would bring me dailies. I'd be the biggest slacker in the entire company. And I would lead the drinking songs by the pool until we all passed out on the deck.

I heave a sigh.

I can do none of that.

Instead, I change into conservative blue swim trunks and a white T-shirt.

Perhaps to make up for this, I'll convince my brother Court to go on a singles cruise with me. We'll insist on *twenty* fingerprints for our rooms and use each and every one.

I stop in the bathroom and muss my hair slightly. In this outfit, I look like myself. Rhett Amstrong, player, fun-lover, weekend beach bum.

But for the next four days, I'll have to shove that part of me deep into a hole.

Time for the boss to write a speech.

And *definitely* not think about Bailey Johansson.

5

———

BAILEY

The room inspection was an idle threat. They never intended to barge in.

I wait long, excruciating minutes, then push the chair away from the desk. My legs are cramped from my tight position, and I flail across the floor in a chaos of pink sundress and screaming limbs.

I lie on the carpet, staring at the beautiful tin ceiling. Is this worth it?

It will be. I picture the sandy beach, the ocean water lapping over my ankles.

Yes. I will get there.

I drag myself to standing, desperately wishing I'd packed some snacks. The horizon remains an unbroken blue of water and sky.

By lunch, I am starving. The itinerary left on the desk says that after the champagne send-off and mustering, there is a poolside welcome by, of course, my nemesis Rhett Armstrong. I have to skip that.

Then a lunch buffet is set up from noon to two.

I figure everyone will dash there right away, so if I sneak down at, let's say, one o'clock, it will be quiet.

The mirror assures me that my oversized sunglasses and floppy sun hat are a good disguise. My chestnut hair with its distinctive purple highlights is completely hidden.

My sundress is colorful, but otherwise loose and not something that makes you look twice. The flip-flops are generic. My poor Bernie Mevs. One is still much pinker than the other.

I've even glossed my nails with beige. I'm here to fly under the radar, eat free food, lounge in the pool, and see the sights. This trip is owed to me for my two years of service to the evil one. I'm going to savor every minute.

And not get caught until it's too late for Rhett to do anything about it.

By the time I creep down the hall to the main deck and peer out across the pool area, I'm light-headed with hunger. There's a collection of tables and chairs near the buffet, covered with a blue-and-white striped awning and watched over by two crew members.

The Dougherty employees are scattered about. Some are in the pool, drink in hand. Others bask in the sun, including Marney from marketing, who has finally shucked her orthopedics.

No one in the vicinity of the food would recognize me straight away. No Viola. No marketing or accounting people I dealt with daily.

I don't think most employees would recognize me at a glance, even though it was my job to know them. I always had to help Rhett, who couldn't hold a personal detail about another human if he tried. I don't know what makes Rhett smile, but it isn't anyone or anything at Dougherty Inc. I was the one who exclaimed over baby pictures, listened to long descriptions of vacations, and congratulated people on engagements.

Rhett is not a people person. He's a big ol' fuddy duddy and never stops working.

I walk casually along the wall, avoiding all eye contact. Hopefully, anyone glancing my way will assume I'm a wife or girlfriend of an employee and look elsewhere.

The smell of the food hits me, and the ground briefly swoops out from under me. I haven't had so much as a coffee since I got up and rushed to the cruise dock.

No one is in line at the buffet, so I approach the stack of large white plates and pick one up. It's a dizzying array of Caribbean food. Jerk chicken. Rice. Plantains with dipping sauces in green, red, and yellow. Empanadas.

"What would you like, love?" The woman's smooth dark skin is as flawless as a Cover Girl ad.

"One of everything?" I ask.

She grins. "We can manage that." She adds a hefty serving of the steaming chicken, several fried plantains, a spoonful of rice, and a golden-brown empanada. Each of the sauces is artfully ladled between the dishes.

"Some salad?" The next woman holds tongs over a

bowl of gorgeous greens mixed with slivers of vegetables I don't even recognize, glistening with a light oil dressing.

"Yes, please."

I'm handed a bowl of it by a smiling woman who says, "The bar across the way has water, Goombay Punch, and adult beverages."

"Goombay Punch?" For some random reason, Rhett's secret nickname, "Mr. Juicy," pops into my head.

"It's a popular Bahamian soda."

I glance over at the bar. It's a dangerous place, surrounded by at least six people I talked to most every day.

"Thank you."

I don't need a drink at the moment. I just need to eat.

I find a small table at the edge of the cluster of seats. I debate turning my back on the pool to avoid identification, then decide I should keep an eye on anyone approaching.

I eat the salad first, that swoony feeling coming over me again at the variety of flavors in the tangy vinaigrette. No one has noticed me, so I dip my first plantain into the green sauce.

It's heavenly, a touch sweet with a heavy dose of cilantro. I'm very glad I'm not one of those people for whom cilantro tastes like soap.

The red sauce is so spicy that I have to eat rice to tone it down. Then the jerk chicken fills my mouth with a warm, toasty flavor with a bite at the end.

I calm down with the food and take in everyone on

the main deck. I spot Viola in the hot tub, standing out in a bright pink bikini. Kenna sits on the rim, only her feet in the water, nodding mindlessly at Viola's chatter.

That used to be my job.

A pang hits me that I got trodden so hard by my so-called best friend, and yet I still miss her. Viola is that moderately toxic friend you know you ought to quit, and yet her light shines so brightly, you're drawn to her anyway. Life was never boring with her around.

But she got me fired. I wonder if she did such a good snow job on whatever marketing disaster she got me blamed for that it will never be undone. It's been two weeks, so I assume that while she was mediocre at marketing, she was excellent at sabotage.

And for what? Rhett? My job? Is that what she wanted? I was never clear. All I know is that she made a stray comment that she thought Rhett was looking at me more than he ought to, then BOOM, two days later, I'm called into HR.

There wasn't much I could question without a deep dive. Every requisition I was presented with had Rhett's signature on it, and my initials showing that I'd given it to him to sign. But he was the boss, so he wasn't going to be the one to get fired over a half-million in useless expenditures, all uncovered by Viola and a shocked Marney.

No, that would be me.

I look down at my empty plate, surprised to see I've eaten everything but the fiery red sauce. I contemplate returning for a second helping when I spot Gina from

HR strolling toward the buffet. Her trajectory will take her perilously close to my table.

I glance around for a bussing bin, but a member of the crew swoops in. "All finished, my lady?" asks a handsome young man in a blue vest and white shirt.

"Yes." Before he can even make away with my plate, I've launched from my chair and headed away from the buffet. I can always come back later for more.

I beeline for the railing on the opposite side of the deck, the rows of lounge chairs mostly empty other than a snoozing Alaina from operations.

The boat glides through the Atlantic, an occasional spray rising high enough to sprinkle cool droplets on my arms and cheeks. There is nothing as far as the eye can see in any direction, only unbroken ocean and the vast open sky.

Now, this is why I snuck onto the cruise. I close my eyes to the afternoon light, dazzling even through my sunglasses. I lean my arms on the cool rail and soak it all in. Everything falls away. My lost job. My bills, which will stack up soon, unpaid. My traitorous former best friend.

Gone.

It's all good now, the boat sluicing through the water, the sun warming my face. Today is about delicious food and time to myself.

Tomorrow I'll have sandy beaches and drinks with umbrellas and reading to the sound of waves lapping the shore.

Life is good. I will be fine. There will be other jobs. With better bosses. A new bestie. I will survive this.

I let out a long, slow exhale. In this moment, I am happy. Content.

Then I hear a familiar voice.

"Good God, Bailey, is that you?"

6

RHETT

Finally, some peace and quiet.

I requested a plate be sent to my cabin rather than eat lunch with the rest of the company. I got plenty of employee time during the welcome party.

It took a lot of restraint when the bar opened not to step right up. But drinking is a slippery slope. Once I get started, party Rhett might come out to play.

Instead, I open the binders Gloria brought while I sample an incredible selection of Caribbean food. I savor each one for a moment. The green sauce on plantains is pure bliss.

But work eventually calls. I'm particularly interested in the marketing requisitions. I've barely gotten started when there's a knock on my door.

What now?

I peer through the peephole.

Great. Viola Jennings has figured out which cabin is mine.

"I see the shadow behind the peephole!" Her voice grates on my last nerve.

I gather my patience and put on my sternest expression before opening the door.

"Yes, Viola?"

"All work and no play makes Rhett a dull boss." She saunters right past me, her white mesh swimsuit cover-up falling off her shoulders to gather at her elbows. Her damp flip-flops leave footprints on the carpet.

She glances around. "Huh. I thought your suite would be huge." She heads to my balcony. "This is bigger, though. I can barely squeeze this backside onto mine." She tosses a saucy look over her shoulder. Her assets are barely contained in a pink bikini, easily seen through the mesh. She knows it. She's working it.

"Can I help you, Viola?"

She spots the leather books. "Are you working? I thought you were just in hiding!" Her eyes narrow at the dailies. "You had all this printed out?"

"Is there something I can do for you?" I struggle to keep my tone civil.

"Come for a swim. You're all dressed for it. You ran off after your speech like a frightened rabbit."

A rabbit. She called me a rabbit. My jaw clenches. I want her out of here. I've kept very strict rules about my office door for years, only to have them all thrown out the window in mere hours on this cruise. Now I have an employee alone with me in a cabin.

"How did you know which room was mine?"

"I knocked on every door. You're the only one holing up."

Good God. "I appreciate your concern. I will be on the island tomorrow with everyone else. Until then, I am not at quite the level of leisure as the rest of you."

She turns the page of one of the books. "Yes, that's perfectly clear. Okay. But I expect to see you tomorrow." She closes the book, making me lose my place.

I'm not sure what has made her think it's appropriate to be this bold with me, and I don't like it. I open the door. "See you tomorrow, Viola."

"All right. I can take a hint." She heads for the hall. "But tomorrow."

I close the door. This cruise is going to be more difficult than I thought.

Not that I'm tempted by Viola. She's not my type at all. Colorful and loud is more my brother Court's speed. Actually, everyone is his type. He's for any port in a storm. He likes to say all cats are gray in the dark.

I'm a bit more discerning.

I've barely sat down again when there's another knock. Is she back already? I've learned my lesson about the peephole and don't bother to get up.

But after a moment there's another knock, then Gloria's tentative voice. "Mr. Armstrong?"

I stride to the door. Gloria is slightly disheveled, her cheeks pink from the sun, her graying hair wild from being wet, then air-dried.

"Is everything all right?"

"I'm so sorry to bother you. I made it my aim to leave you alone as much as possible." She twists her wedding ring.

"Is something wrong?"

"It's the satellite feed. Did you check it?"

"Not yet."

"I'm afraid they won't be able to get it up and running until we stop in Freeport. Something about the receiver getting an electrical surge."

"On a ship this expensive, they can't get their satellite feed to work?"

"I'm just the messenger." Gloria's face flushes red.

"All right. Thank you for letting me know. I hope we don't have any emergencies while we're all here." Damn it all. I knew this was a bad idea. When Uncle Sherman lets me have it over the marketing snafu, I'm going to give as good as I get about *this* fiasco.

"I guess we won't rightly know, now will we?" Gloria forces a smile. "Do try to enjoy yourself, Mr. Armstrong. Everyone is looking to you for the tone of the trip."

This gets me. Uncle Sherman's direct order was to make sure this was a lively affair. "Isn't everyone having fun? There were plenty of drinks getting served at the welcome party."

"I get the sense some of them are holding back, like you might fire them if they cut loose. Will you be there for karaoke? That might liven things up."

I could. The Pickles are notorious for their karaoke. It's a big feature of the yearly gathering of the deli managers. I've attended several of those through the years, even though I've never worked at one of the family restaurants myself.

I have a couple of karaoke numbers I've worked up should I get forced on stage by family. One is a swinging rendition of "Hello, Dolly" that always makes people laugh. And then there's my take on "You Look Wonderful Tonight" that will usually get me the girl.

But party Rhett is not the Rhett I can be here.

"I don't think it's a good look for the boss," I say.

"All right," she says. "I understand." She hesitates. "A lot of people at Dougherty say you're made of stone. But I know better." She turns to hurry down the hall.

So, people say I'm made of stone.

I guess I really have played the boss.

But maybe I've taken the role too far. I was hard on Bailey. I had my reasons.

I turn back to the binders. There's no fixing this problem. I'm in charge. I have to keep the ship afloat.

And right now, that's both figurative *and* literal.

7

BAILEY

Oh, no. It's Kenna, Viola's new bestie.

I don't turn away from the rail of the ship. My insides flash hot, like someone's set off a sparkler in my chest.

But we're in the middle of the ocean. I can see that from all sides. What can anyone do to me now?

I spin to face her. "Hello, Kenna." I take in her black yoga capris and oversized pink shirt with *Back Off* in huge black letters. I like it.

Her cheeks are flushed. "What are you doing here? Mr. Armstrong fired you weeks ago."

I shrug. "I felt entitled to the trip. So I came."

Her dark eyes go wide, making her pale face and pink cheeks more dramatic. Her brown hair is pulled back so tightly into a ponytail that I can almost hear her follicles crying out in pain. "You really did that?"

I gesture to my pink dress. "I'm here, aren't I?"

"They let you on?" She's still in shock.

"I had a boarding pass. We were issued them before my completely undeserved firing."

"But you cost the company half a million dollars."

That again. "Where's Viola?"

"She went off looking for Mr. Armstrong."

"What for?" Surely she's not going to try to make a move on a company trip.

Kenna shrugs. "She wanted to find his room."

So she *is* going to go for it. She's lost her mind. That man is *not* worth it.

"Is that wise?"

"You know Viola."

I do. And now Kenna does. Jealousy boils in me for a moment. "She dumped me."

"I know."

"So, you two hang out?"

"She needed a ride to work." Kenna braces her elbows on the rail, looking out over the sea. "I'm under no delusions that she actually likes me. But I believe in keeping your enemies close."

"Enemies?"

Her gaze flicks to me, then back to the water. "Nobody should ever treat a friend like she did you."

This conversation is a revelation a minute. "I don't know why she did it. I assume Rhett will figure it out, eventually."

"Figure what out?"

"That there was no way I could have intentionally made a mistake like that. I don't have the experience or authority."

"But you had him sign all the requisitions."

"I brought Rhett a lot of things to sign as his assistant."

"He tossed you right out. Everyone was talking about it."

"I was there." Now it's my gaze that stays on the water.

"He must have believed you were at fault."

"Doesn't make it true."

We sit there a while longer, the waves smashing against the side of the ship. Behind us, the "Chicken Dance" is playing and people must be participating because I hear the *clap-clap-clap-clap* part.

"You're missing all the fun," I tell Kenna.

She whirls around, back against the rail. "I'm not a 'Chicken Dance' kind of girl."

I am, and Viola is. But I can't go out there.

"Are you going to tell Viola I'm here? Or Rhett?"

"No. At least, I don't think so. I probably wouldn't last long in a torture situation."

This makes me laugh. I didn't realize Kenna had such a dry sense of humor.

"Just remember if they handcuff you with duct tape, lift your arms and bring them down fast."

She snorts. "Noted."

I long to turn around and look at the crowd, but I resist. I could get Kenna in trouble, too.

"You probably shouldn't stand with me for long," I say. "It might get noticed."

"Are you going to hide the whole time?"

My gaze follows a sea gull winging over the water.

"No. But I'm delaying the reveal. Maybe on the island tomorrow."

"He's going to be incredibly pissed."

"I know. I'm looking forward to it."

Kenna pushes away from the rail. "Good luck, Bailey."

I remain in position as long as I can stand it. A conga line song plays. I want to be out there, drinking rum runners and whooping it up.

But not yet. I follow my instinct at all times, and it's saying to hang back, hold on a little longer.

The conga song is in full swing, so I figure most everyone will be watching the action. I should make my escape before someone else recognizes me.

I tilt my head, still shielded by the hat.

I look out of the corner of my eye as I head across the deck. Fewer people than I expect are participating, a few wives and girlfriends mainly. The only employee is Peter from maintenance. His wife is the life of the party, leading the line, kicking her legs out from her bright floral swim wrap. I like her.

But other than their paltry conga line, this party is decidedly *not lit*.

Kenna drops onto a lounge chair well away from the others. She glances at me, then quickly looks away.

She's considerably more interesting than I thought she would be. At least Viola has good taste in friends, even if she ultimately screws them over.

I scan every cluster of people. Rhett isn't here, which I'm sure is why Viola went looking for him. Playing with fire. That's her M.O. She had a fling with Toby in tech that went so far south that Toby quit his job.

That was all Viola's doing, constantly sending in IT requests after they broke up and refusing to let any other tech help. Only Toby. Just to torture him.

She's always able to justify her actions in her head. It's impressive. I'm most certainly better off without her, even if it stings.

I thread my way through the dining chairs back to the buffet. I should make a plan in case I chicken out of dinner. It's a sit-down affair in the dining room, and I'm not sure I'm ready for that level of discovery.

The first serving woman grins at me. "Back for more? We're shutting down shortly."

"Can I take some empanadas to my room?"

"Certainly. How many?"

"Three. And some plantains. But not the red sauce."

She laughs. "Too spicy for you?"

"Too spicy for this earth!"

She laughs again. "No red sauce." She fills a cardboard container and sets a package of wooden takeaway cutlery on top. "This good?"

"Perfect. Hey, what else can we get in our rooms?"

"Most anything you like. There's a small binder in your desk that outlines the kitchen and bar options that are included with your stay."

This is a dream. Worth every risk. "Thank you so much." I accept the container.

I keep my head down, glancing left and right as I head for the covered part of the deck that leads to the cabins.

I'm almost to the hall when I see a swish of white net and a pink bikini.

That's Viola. I remember that suit.

I spin to the side and face a large window.

She's focused on where she's going, maybe a little mad, and doesn't even look my way.

I guess things didn't go so well with Rhett. I could have told her. That man doesn't have a fun bone in his body. I've seen most every unattached woman at Dougherty Inc. sidle her way into his office on one pretense or another, and he ushers them out as swiftly as possible.

All of his socials were stalked. We saw a rare picture of him with the Pickle family, but nothing about a girl-friend. Or anything fun. The best we could find was him singing with his cousins on a stage during the Pickle Deli's anniversary party in New York.

Rhett looks way more relaxed with family, that's for sure. Viola dissected every detail of that image, convinced the right party girl would bring out his fun self.

But it hasn't happened. If anything, he's gotten more tightly wound since I've known him. When he and I had private meetings, he took great care to make sure the door was open, like he expected I'll tell some wild story about what we did in there.

As if.

I move quickly down the hall. I'm getting the lay of the land. We came in on a lower deck, level with the dock. This floor is where my cabin is and leads out to the party deck with the pool, buffet, hot tub, and bar.

But there is an upper level, probably with more upscale cabins. I wonder if that's where Rhett is staying.

Doesn't matter. I rush to the safety of my room with my bonus food.

Tonight, I'll enjoy my cabin, take a late stroll in the dark of night, and tomorrow will be the big day that I shock the hell out of Dougherty Inc.

8

───────

RHETT

The next morning dawns bright.

I head to the gym below deck, unsurprised to find it empty at six a.m. The live band played well beyond the midnight buffet.

I worked straight through dinner, reviewing the marketing requisitions. The new company that caused all the fuss didn't deliver much of anything. Half a million going nowhere.

All managed by Bailey, who had ardently championed the new campaign for Dougherty. I remember getting these requisitions.

A new mission statement? A logo redesign that no one asked for? A list of contacts that were primarily defunct? Who was checking the cost against the results?

I trace back the invoices and the deliverables, but I don't have the correspondence, only the numbers and lists. It's not enough information to follow the trail to its source. Hopefully, I got Bailey out of the office fast enough that she wasn't able to delete her email history.

The treadmill hums as it cranks into a higher gear, the mechanism lifting the base at a steep angle. I focus on the workout, keeping the stride strong and sure. I clear my mind, staying present, but the moment the program slides into a recovery pace, my mind is back on it.

Marketing. Money. Bailey.

I can picture her face when I fired her. She seemed to shut down, like she'd expected it to happen. I wanted her to fight me, prove me wrong. But she sank onto the sofa, stunned, like she hadn't planned on anyone catching her.

What was that company she was using? Something owned by a family member? A friend? This mysterious Maxwell?

My hand slams on the bar. Of course. Dougherty Inc. has been funding that lavish lifestyle. It totally makes sense.

I crank the machine into a higher level, running at a punishing pace to burn off my anger. I have zero remorse for firing her.

She'll be doing fine, if Maxwell hasn't spent it all.

Damn it.

Right under my nose.

The treadmill beeps, signaling the end of the program. I consider doing another, but my watch chimes a warning that I have an hour until a small boat will tender us to the private island.

That activity is one I can't ignore, as it's an all-day thing. The island is small, only a mile across. It's owned by Blue Sapphire and is completely undeveloped to make visitors feel like they have escaped the world.

I wrap a towel around my neck and endeavor to set aside my anger at what happened to the company on my watch. In the hallway, I pass several sleepy employees headed to the breakfast buffet on the pool deck. We simply nod in greeting.

I've decided on coffee in my room. I'll do plenty of peopling on the island.

I'm calmer by the time I'm showered and dressed in swim trunks and a Pickle Deli T-shirt that says, "This is a Big Dill." Hopefully, it will seem slightly less rigid while still maintaining my inherent boss-ness.

Made of stone. They have no idea who the real Rhett Armstrong is.

But I'm not exactly able to show them.

When I make it downstairs, the first boat has already filled with eager employees and guests. I stand at the back of the group to wait, but Sarah, the VP of operations, waves at me. "Rhett, come on. We have room for one more."

With a nod from the uniformed man who is ushering people onto the boat, I move through the others with a tight smile, and plenty of "excuse me" and "thank you."

I step over the short lip of the boat, and a man in white lifts the ramp. When he has it secured, he calls out to the main ship, "We'll be back shortly for the second round!"

The small boat is covered with a canvas awning. A long bench lines both sides. Multiple rows of seats in the middle are filled with excited beachgoers.

I sit next to Sarah, not sure I'm thrilled that I ended up jumping the line. But she nudges my shoulder with hers and says, "Lighten up, Rhett."

Her husband Caleb leans forward to talk around her. Their hands are clasped on her red-and-yellow floral swim wrap. He says, "Rhett, good to see you."

"Thanks. Glad you could make it."

"Couldn't miss out on Blue Sapphire. They are both legendary and the biggest secret in celebrity cruises."

Sarah leans her head on his shoulder. "Rhett knows all the good stuff."

I like Sarah. In another life, she and Caleb would be personal friends as well as people I know from work. She was the first person I sought when the Bailey situation broke, and she advised me to respond swiftly. She's usually all business in pencil skirts and reading glasses, but today she'd cuddled close to Caleb, the top of her face shaded blue from a sun visor.

"We missed you at the events last night," she says. "Gloria was unwilling to spill the beans, but I assume you were working."

"Maybe I was doing shots with the captain."

She snorts so hard with a laugh that Caleb pounds her back. "Now this is the guy I want to party with," he says.

I don't hear that often at Dougherty. I glance to see if anyone is listening. A few people look our way, but the roar of the engine makes it impossible for sound to carry. I can't hear any conversation beyond Sarah and Caleb. On the other side of me is nothing but the man steering the boat.

"I hear there will be all the margaritas you can drink on the island," Sarah says. "And floaters of every flavor."

"One of each, right, baby?" Caleb kisses her forehead.

Their closeness makes my solitude more acute. Dating has been nearly impossible these last few years, other than the random hookups when hanging out with Axel and Court. Or just Court now, since Axel seems to have settled.

Caleb reaches behind Sarah to poke my shoulder. "I challenge you to a tequila shot war."

I hold up my hand at that. "Come now. Somebody has to be in charge."

Sarah shakes her head. "You can take Rhett out of the office, but you can't take the office out of Rhett."

If she'd known me before Dougherty, she would never have said that. But Uncle Sherman was a man on a mission when our generation of the Pickle clan started having kids. He turned the delis over to his sons and put all his energy into these side businesses to bring on any extended family who wanted in.

I was given Dougherty.

Court became a VP of Pickle Media. Axel was already deep into his hiking app, which later sold for a cool half-million, so he's doing this own thing in Colorado.

Our sister Nadia has also eluded the lure of the Pickle empire, although the way she and Uncle Sherman holed up together last Christmas makes me wonder if they're working on something.

Water splashes the side of the boat, getting several people wet. They let out a cheer, as if the party has started. The island grows nearer. Its pristine sand lines the shore, dotted with blue chairs and backed with palm trees.

There isn't much to it. Blue Sapphire employees stand on the end of the dock, where another, smaller boat is moored. We approach the opposite side and a crew member on the boat tosses a thick rope toward a man at the end of the wood planks.

In moments, they have both ends of the boat secured against the side of the dock. A short set of stairs is moved to the front, and most of the IT department, who apparently all loaded together, starts climbing out.

I wait for the others to disembark, taking in the shore.

The dock ends on the beach. A woman waits with a cart filled with colorful beach towels, handing them to everyone who passes.

To the right is a long hut with rough-hewn wood planks and a thatched roof. The front side is open, and staff members in bright blue shorts and T-shirts unpack food to rest on trays of ice.

Nestled behind it is another thatched hut with doors marked Women and Men. Bathrooms, I presume.

A good-sized shed, this one with a metal roof, has its doors thrown open. Outside of it are racks of life jackets and oars. Rows of red kayaks and standing paddle boats line the beach on that end.

The members of IT are already hustling to claim

the blue beach chairs, tossing their towels over the backs. This place will be considerably less serene by the time the entire company is ashore.

I wonder if I could grab a kayak and stay out in the water all day, but Sarah grabs my arm and steers me to the food hut. "First, margaritas," she says.

And me with nothing but coffee so far.

I shouldn't have worried. There is so much food inside the hut that I could stave off hunger for a month. I load a half-dozen oysters onto a plate while Sarah and Caleb marvel over the hand-crank margarita machine.

I join them, watching the young man put all his muscle into the oversized metal handle that turns the ice shaver.

"By the time you get a margarita, you've burned off the calories," she says.

The slushy ice falls into a large bowl. A woman with her hair pulled into two spunky buns dumps the ice into a huge glass pitcher partially filled with golden margarita mix. She then squeezes several limes into the pale gold liquid.

Then she lifts the pitcher and gives it a hard shake.

The results are magnificent, a frothy, slushy frozen margarita at just the right thickness. She pours the pitcher out into a row of paper cups. "Take what you like!"

Sarah passes one to me. "Bottoms up, boss."

We clink our cups.

This is good. I take a sip, marveling at the gorgeousness of the drink.

I'm with people I like. The food is good. The drinks are great. The beach is nice. And I've escaped the nightmare of the Bailey Johannson fiasco for a while.

Maybe this day will be all right.

9

BAILEY

The time to get caught is at hand.

We have to take a small boat to the island, and we'll be seated tightly together. There will be nowhere to hide.

I watch the process from my balcony. Rhett got on the first boat. I saw him step across.

But the bulk of that group was IT, maintenance, and operations. That means marketing, finance, and HR will be on my boat. All the people I know best.

I draw in a deep breath. It's showtime.

My outfit is glorious, bought just for this occasion. A black two-piece and a white cover-up with red poppies. My sun hat matches with a bright red band, and my red flip-flops slap against my feet as I hurry down the hall to the stairs. I plan to follow everyone onto the boat in the very back.

I have a straw bag packed with sunscreen, a water bottle, and a few sand sculpting tools from my childhood.

I love to make sand castles. Growing up in Florida, I had a blast winning against older kids in the competitions. I can make a very convincing Taj Mahal, although I most love carving sweet cottages with picket fences and flower gardens.

Besides, I'm expecting a shunning, so I'll need something to do. I tuck my phone in the bag, even though it won't have a signal. I can still use it to take pictures.

There will be excellent food, margaritas, sun, and surf. What else do I need?

I hurry down the stairs. It would totally suck to miss the boat. I would not have nearly as good a time alone on a cruise ship. I'm here for the private beach without the crowd of strangers like the ones near Miami.

And if I'm honest with myself, I know that I'm hoping someone will talk to me and I can clear my name. Having all the employees from Dougherty Inc. stuck with me on an island is the opportunity I never got when Rhett fired me.

By the time I arrive at the lowest level of the ship, the second group is shuffling toward the open side, carefully stepping into the half-full boat.

I assess the situation. Viola and Kenna are already sitting at the back, hands shielding their eyes as they gaze out at the not-too-distant island. I read about it last night. It's too shallow for the yacht to get close to shore, so we have to take a small boat called a *tender* to its private dock.

There's no electricity once we get there, and the bathrooms use a specialized gravity-based plumbing system for the toilets and outdoor showers to wash off sand.

I bounce on my feet to settle my nerves. Everyone's back is to me, so nobody looks my way as they get onto the boat. I adjust my sunglasses, drawing in a long breath to slow my hammering heart.

I only need a few minutes more. If they see me too soon, I could get loaded back onto the yacht to be dealt with. But if we're already headed to the island, I feel certain we'll make it there. At that point, they'll take me to Rhett.

Am I ready for that?

Only five people are left to load ahead of me, and of course they would include Marney from marketing and Gina from HR, both of whom know me well.

I tilt my head down, using the hat as a shield. I have to make it.

When it's my turn to step on, several people are looking my way. I aim my face toward the front of the boat and quickly sit on a bench near the captain. Panic rises in me. I imagine an entire legion of Dougherty Inc. employees swinging me back and forth, then tossing me to the sharks.

My breathing speeds up. I press my hand to my chest.

The captain turns to me quizzically. "Everything okay?"

"Not so much."

"Anything I can do?"

I turn to him. He's dark-skinned with friendly eyes

and a well-trimmed beard. Would he help? It doesn't hurt to ask. "Is it possible to create a diversion so people won't stare at me?"

He tilts his head, then miraculously says, "You've got it."

He lifts a palm-sized mouthpiece and presses the button. His voice reverberates out of speakers attached to the canopy. "Welcome aboard the Mini Sapphire, porting you directly from the ship to our private island paradise. If you'll look behind you, you can see the white sandy beaches of the island. Keep your eyes on the water because sometimes dolphins will ride beside the boat. Get your phones out so you don't miss them."

He sets the microphone down with a wink. "That'll keep 'em busy."

"Are there lots of dolphins?"

He chuckles. "Not here."

Oh, a wild goose chase. Even better. "Thank you."

He starts the engine, and we pull away from the yacht. I hold my hat as we speed up. The wind blows my hair in every direction, and the light spray of the water is cool and refreshing.

I steal a glance behind me. Allen from operations is pointing at something in the water, and everyone has their phones aimed at it. I bite back a smile. Funny how a total stranger can be an ally, and the people you thought were your closest friends can betray you in the worst way.

Sitting in the front of the boat is like flying. We skim across the rolling waves, occasionally bumping enough that I briefly leave my seat.

The panic washes away. I want to laugh out loud, sing into the wind, get up and dance. I've done it. I'm here! Rhett can't take away the feeling I have right now. The trouble has disappeared, and there is nothing but sunshine, blue water, and a gorgeous day ahead.

I haven't felt this happy in a very long time. In fact, the last time I remember feeling this way, I was on the beach with my dad making a sand replica of the 1986 Corvette he owned when he graduated high school.

We finished the tail lights and sat back to look at it.

"We make a great team, Bailey-boo," he said. "You're the best sand crafter I've ever known."

The sun was warm that day, and the beach was quiet. We ate hot dogs and chips with sandy hands, and I remember thinking, the world is mine. I'd just found out I'd been accepted to Florida State, and my life seemed so full of promise.

Today has that same external feeling. Sun. Ocean. Victory.

But all good things do end. The motor throttles down, and we approach the dock. The employees who took the first boat have settled on beach chairs or are wading along the shore.

There will be no escaping detection the minute we all stand up. The step out of the boat is right beside me.

The driver tosses a rope to one of the crew members, and they pull the boat to align with the dock. Behind me, everyone gathers their things to stand.

I might as well make a dramatic reveal. It's the Bailey way.

I draw in a deep breath, turn around, and pull my hat off my head.

As everyone moves toward me to exit the boat, I call out, "Hi, everyone! Long time, no see!"

10

RHETT

After three margaritas, this trip isn't half bad.

Sarah, Caleb, and I drag beach chairs a solid hundred feet from the others and drink, eat, and laugh.

Sarah, it turns out, is excellent at impressions. She's nailed Gina from HR, and it's a riot.

She lowers her voice and takes on a stern expression. "And those time cards are due precisely at five p.m. Not five-o-one. I like to get home for a weekend too, you know."

Caleb and I laugh and laugh.

I'm on my fourth plate of oysters, and the sun, booze, and surf are working their magic. I can scarcely remember why I felt like I had to be so straitlaced at work.

It's amazing being me.

I'm the big boss. I call the shots.

Take that, Bailey Johansson.

But I can picture her, the way she would sit at her desk, her head cocked as she stared at the computer monitor. She liked to bend the straw of her boba tea toward her, even though that often meant the pearls got stuck.

There was the way she jumped a little whenever anyone disturbed her, like she was so deep in concentration that the office had ceased to exist. And she would always let out a light, tinkling laugh afterward, like she was so silly for having gotten startled.

Every day after lunch, she would reapply a pale pink gloss on her lips. I could see her desk from mine when the door was open. She had a tiny mirror in her purse, and she would hold it with her left hand, apply the gloss with her right, then press her lips together.

She always made a *pop* sound with her mouth, then narrowed her eyes at her own reflection, as if she didn't quite appreciate what she saw there.

"Hey." Caleb elbows me. "I'm going to cool off. You want to go in?"

I lift my margarita. "And let this melt?"

"Glad to see you have your priorities straight." Caleb hauls himself off his chair and runs out into the waves. Sarah and I watch him high step it into the water, then dive beneath the surface.

"You're lucky," I tell her.

She searches for the straw a moment with her mouth before finding it and taking a sip. We're all three sheets to the wind.

Then she says, "How so?"

I gesture out to where Caleb is swimming parallel with the beach. "Great job. Great relationship. You didn't let half a million get siphoned out of the company."

"You handled it."

I did. No more boba tea straws or lip gloss. But even with all the drinks, I know not to say that out loud. "I haven't been called on it yet."

Sarah turns toward me. Her cheeks are pink from the sun. "Does Dougherty know?"

Even Sarah doesn't know Dougherty is my Uncle Sherman. "No."

"When will you tell him?"

This work talk is bringing down my buzz. "When we get back."

She drops her legs over the side of the lounger to sit up. Now she's serious. "Do you think your position is in danger?"

"No." Ha. My uncle practically made this company for me. I suppress the words so I won't say them out loud.

"Has anything like this happened before?" Sarah is new, only six months in the position. I created it as we expanded.

I work very hard to sound serious. "No. I guess it's a risk of growing as rapidly as we did."

"We might need more oversight. Shouldn't accounting have caught this?"

I struggle to make a sentence sound business-like. "It was a natural progression of the marketing budget. They only look at numbers, not the qualitative piece."

Sarah peers into her cup. "Will you bring this up with Dougherty?"

"Certainly."

She swirls her paper straw. "Did you know Dougherty before the start-up?"

Uh oh. We're getting into dangerous territory for the amount of alcohol I've consumed. I am absolutely not allowed to reveal the family connection. I'll have to watch my loose mouth.

"I did." Good. Short and sweet.

Thankfully, Caleb returns, dripping in every direction.

"Hey!" Sarah pulls her cup out of the splash zone. "Don't water down my drink!"

He grins at her and shakes like a dog, sending droplets flying.

I throw a towel at him, laughing. That's more like it. We were getting way too serious with the work talk.

Caleb settles back on his lounger. "Fetch me a fresh drink, woman! Mine is all melted!"

Sarah narrows her eyes at him and pours her margarita on his chest.

"Hey! Now I'm sticky!" He scoops the slush into his hand and licks it.

Sarah shoves him away from her. "Gross! Get back in the water and wash it off!"

Caleb grins at her. "You lick it off."

I down my drink, jealousy spiking through me. I want this. The relationship. The playfulness. I have to look away.

But when I turn my head toward the huts, I spot Gloria trudging through the sand, a worried expression on her face. Her flowery cover-up flies behind her in the breeze, and her gray hair is a tangle of curls. She's headed in our direction.

"Uh oh," Sarah says. "We're gonna get busted by HR."

"Shhh," Caleb says. "You talk too much when you're drunk."

"You talk too loud."

Gloria stops next to my chair. "Mr. Armstrong?"

I sit up on the lounger. "Why so glum, Gloria? It's vacation! Have a margarita! Slurp some oysters."

Her lips pinch into a frown. "I'm allergic."

"To alcohol?"

"To shellfish."

I move my plate to the opposite side of the chair to be farther from her. "There are other choices. But get the Midori floater on your margarita. It's perfect."

Something flickers on her face. "I'm very glad to see you having fun finally, Mr. Armstrong, but I have some distressing news."

I wave her off. "The satellite is down, Gloria. If the company is falling apart, we won't even know it. You said so yourself." I lift my empty cup to Caleb. He fills it again from the pitcher, then tries to clink my cup with his, misses, and instead clinks it with the pitcher.

"To broken satellites," he says.

"Damn straight." My drink sloshes slightly, so I lick it off the back of my hand. It's gritty with sand.

"Oh, dear," Gloria says. "Maybe I should let it go for the moment."

Sarah stands at that, holds out her arms, and in a loud, bell-like voice, sings, "Let it go!"

Caleb and I join her. "Let it go!"

Gloria takes several steps back. "Okay, Mr. Armstrong. I will." She shakes her head. "You should have done that number at karaoke."

"I still might!"

But as I watch her retreating figure, something nags at the back of my mind. Work. Appearances. Distance.

I'm supposed to maintain a stiff demeanor. Keep myself separate.

But then a Blue Sapphire crew member arrives with a plate of tacos and yet another pitcher of frothy margaritas, and I forget all about it.

11

BAILEY

I didn't expect quite this much screeching.

So many people head toward me in the little boat that it starts to tilt.

The captain scrambles to get on the microphone. "Do not cram the front of the vessel! Please spread out and exit in an orderly fashion."

Sweat beads on his forehead. He's really freaking out.

Nobody listens. Gina from HR pushes through the gawking crowd. "Bailey Johansson, what in the world are you doing on this boat?"

The murmuring gets louder. The captain turns to me. "Is this about you?"

I nod. "Sorry."

He takes my arm and pulls me behind him. "Everyone, off this boat, now!"

I cower behind his broad form. Maybe hiding is a better plan. We're really tilting. The crew on the dock motions for people to come forward, forcing smiles. A few Dougherty employees head up the steps and out of the boat.

But Gina stands in the cross section of the aisles, leaving a good chunk of the group blocked. "You can't be here! You're not allowed on this trip! This is a huge liability."

The captain stays between me and Gina. "Ma'am, please exit the boat."

Gina won't relent. "You have to take her back! She can't be with us!"

I peer over his shoulder. Gina's face is bright red.

Aaron, the marketing intern, gets frustrated and tries to go around her. But he jostles Marney's husband, who stumbles, his leg ramming the side bench.

His arms wave in wide circles as he loses his balance due to the steep angle of the boat. In seconds, he's let out a "Heeeeey," and toppled over the rail with a splash.

"Jerry!" Marney rushes to the rail, but the tilt is significant, and she can't stop her momentum. Suddenly, she's over the rail, too!

"Damn it." The captain throws his hat on his seat, snags a life saver from a hook near the front, and dives over the edge.

Oh. This is not good.

"See what you did!" Gina cries. "You killed Marney and her husband."

The crew gets more forceful, pulling people off the boat. I turn away from them, pinning my hat to my head, and peer over the edge.

Marney and Jerry bob in the water. The captain swims over to them and hooks their arms over the floating ring. The three of them slowly make their way to the dock, where a long ladder dips into the sea.

"Come on along, thank you, come on along," sing-songs a woman on the dock, trying to force everyone to head to the beach. "We'll take good care of them."

Marney heaves herself up onto the rungs, but Jerry has difficulty.

The captain grunts with the effort of trying to shove Jerry high enough to get a foot on the ladder. He keeps going underwater. The crowd on the boat lets out a gasp every time he dips below the surface.

"Please make your way to the beach," a crew member insists, herding most of marketing down the dock. They crane their necks to watch the struggle in the water.

I stay on the boat as long as possible, watching the Dougherty employees slowly get forced away from the end of the dock. The crew is physically pushing them.

Marney reaches the top of the ladder, and a man hauls her onto the wood planks.

Then it takes the man from above and the boat captain from below to push Jerry's hefty body up to the dock.

I swear half the ocean cascades off him to drench the captain one more time.

A female crew member touches my arm. "We need you to exit the boat."

"This is my fault."

She shakes her head. "No, they refused to listen to the crew."

"But I started it."

"Everything will be fine. Let's get you onto the dock." She leads me off the small boat.

Most of the employees are gone, but Gina waits for me, hands on her hips.

When I get close, she resumes her tirade. "You were fired, missy. You did not have clearance to come on this trip. You're a stowaway and with the cost of each cabin, it's probably a felony act of fraud!"

She doesn't scare me, truly. There's no way Dougherty wants the ugly publicity of me getting arrested or sued or whatever. Once, when we really *did* have fraud, a guy in IT stealing an entire order of iPads totaling fifteen grand, they handled it internally.

So I shrug. "Some people would say it was an act of cruelty to fire me right before a company trip for something that wasn't fully investigated."

Gina is so shocked that I have argued with her about this that she sputters for a bit. I walk past her down the dock.

A crew member hands me a towel. She smiles, but her eyes dart to Gina and back to me.

"Thanks," I tell her, and take one. I'm going to enjoy myself if it kills me.

I aim for the food hut to grab a plate and a margarita, but my confrontations are far from over. Viola is waiting near a pair of blue beach chairs, her eyes like lasers as she watches me walk off the dock.

Here we go.

She tromps toward me in a bright yellow bikini. She must have fake-tanned last night because she's significantly darker than yesterday.

I decide to speak first. "Hello, Viola. I like your suit."

"Don't flatter me, Bailey. I always hated it."

Did she?

"You got fired. What are you doing here?" Her face is flushed, from anger or the heat, I don't know.

"I came anyway. Now, if you'll excuse me, I hear a margarita calling my name."

She holds out a hand to stop me. "You can't do that. You're not an employee. You're not supposed to be here!"

"And yet, here I am." Honestly, this is getting tiring. "Just chill about it, Viola. I snuck onto the boat and nobody can do anything about it."

"They can arrest you when you get off the boat!"

I push past her. "I'm going to risk it."

She lets out a huff. Just past her, Kenna stands in a full-on scuba diving suit. She's pressing her lips together like she can barely hold back her laugh.

I like her. I am always willing to admit when I've misjudged someone, and Kenna is awesome.

The food hut is crowded with people from the second boat. I hang back near the outside corner in the shade and take a moment to figure out where my danger zones are.

Gina is on the dock, talking to a dripping Marney and Jerry. The captain is wringing out his shirt, a puddle forming at his feet. The towel woman walks toward them.

Viola stands where I left her, glaring at me. She turns to Kenna and waves for her to follow, but Kenna shakes her head and points to her suit. Then Kenna takes off toward the kayaks.

This annoys Viola even more. Her hands tighten into fists. I want to laugh. She's a toddler, not getting her way.

But then Gloria, the head of HR, exits the food hut, a plate of food in hand. She's not surprised to see me at all.

"Bailey, sit with me a moment," she says, and her tone is so serious, I follow her without argument.

She settles on a lounger and perches her plate on the belly of her red one-piece. "I apologize for Gina's outburst. She wanted to talk to you first, and I should have known better. This is a situation for me to handle."

I don't want to take the empty chair she's probably saving for her husband, so I kneel in the sand, setting my bag next to me. There's nothing for me to say, so I simply wait.

"I admit I don't like how your termination was handled, and I agree with you that it was incredibly unfair that you were cut out of this company vacation when people like Carl, who has worked here less than a month, got a spot."

Okay, this is going differently than I expected.

She catches a wood fork before it slides off her plate. "I know you were a wonderful assistant to Rhett. I've been doing your job since you left, while we try to find a replacement. You were organized, and I had no trouble picking up your tasks."

A compliment. Also unexpected. "Thank you."

"You won't be thanking me in a minute." She

contemplates her plate, as if wishing she could eat it now. "I have to let Rhett know you are here. You understand that, right?"

"I do."

"I'm not sure how he will react."

"He won't arrest me."

She fiddles with the edge of a taco. Salsa is leaking out of it. "This is a company issue, not one for law enforcement. But there will be consequences."

"I don't know what he can do to me that he hasn't already done. I lost my job. I have no references since this was my first position out of college. I'm screwed."

"You can always have us validate your length of employment and your salary with your next company. We aren't allowed to say anything else."

Oh. I didn't know that.

"But you know he's going to want to talk to you." She hesitates. "And I don't think it will be pretty."

"What won't be pretty?" Gloria's burly husband eases onto the lounger, trying to avoid spilling his load. I try not to stare at the bear-like gray hair furring his chest.

"Nothing important, dear, just a little work concern." Gloria accepts the margarita he hands her, and I marvel at his agility in carrying a plate and two drinks. Find a man who can carry food and two frozen cocktails to you on a beach.

"When will you talk to Rhett?" I ask.

"Not before I eat this," she says. "Find yourself a quiet spot and have a moment. You'll know when he knows."

I bet I will. The roar will probably carry all the way to the Bahamas.

I stand up and brush the sand off my knees. "Thank you, Gloria." I want to petition my case, ask if anyone has looked into the actual fraud, but I don't want to disturb her lunch. There's a lot of trip left to work on that.

As long as Rhett Armstrong doesn't toss me to the sharks when he finds out.

And that will be soon—the amount of time it takes Gloria to eat a taco.

12

———

RHETT

I must fall asleep in the sun because I dream about rain. I startle awake, realizing Caleb is squeezing his shirt on my face.

Now, it really *is* like being with my brothers.

"I hope you wore sunscreen, bro, or you are going to look like a lobster," he says. "Sarah and I are going to hit the kayaks. You wanna come?"

I consider it for a moment. I shield my eyes and peer at the far end of the beach, past the chairs, the dock, and the food hut, to the kayak shack.

It seems quite a few people have gotten the same idea, and that part of the shore is littered with employees pumping oars through the waves.

"That's all right. I'll hang out here."

"All right. Should I tell them to bring you more drinks?" Caleb slings his towel over his shoulder. Sarah is packing her beach bag.

"Nah. I'll switch to water." A dull ache pounds in my head. Crime and punishment. It's already happening.

Sarah passes my chair. "You sure you want to be over here alone? We can move the loungers closer to the rest of the group."

"That's okay. I could use the space."

Caleb scoops up his flip-flops. "Okey-dokey, boss man. Catch you on the other side."

The two of them trudge through the sand, laughing and bumping into each other on purpose.

I lean my head back. What I could really use right now is some Advil.

Bailey would have packed some for me. She was good at predicting little things like that when I had meetings. Late-night session? She'd put chocolate-covered espresso beans in my briefcase. Eating sushi for a lunch meeting? She knew I would be hungry two hours later and would order a sandwich to come to my office midafternoon.

Her again.

I cross my arm over my eyes. The sun is high and hot. I should get wet, maybe. Cool off.

My feet sink into the wet sand as I approach the water. It's shallow for a good twenty feet before notice-ably dropping off. I wade out a ways, then dive below the surface.

The water is clear and pale blue. My arms propel me along the ocean floor, sandy and smooth. A shadow of something catches my eye and I move toward it, bobbing up for a breath, then diving again.

It's a starfish, the size of my hand, resting on the bottom.

I reach out and run my fingers over its bumpy

surface. It pays me no mind. I wonder for a moment if perhaps it's dead, but then I spot the tiny noodle-like feet beneath the star, shifting as it subtly moves. Then the entire tip of one of its limbs twists slightly, as if saying hello.

Something breaks open inside me, this creature, this beautiful island, this peace.

I run my thumb gently along its back in farewell, then push on.

I take another breath and swim along the shallows, wishing for snorkeling equipment. I will make do.

The ocean bottom becomes rockier, and bits of kelp float out from the dark spaces in between. I swim around a more complex outcropping, and suddenly, a school of slender fish with yellow fins darts past me.

I pause, letting them go by, marveling at their speed and how they instinctively stay together, even when making a sharp change in direction.

Another larger, long fish follows in their wake.

It's paradise. I keep going, discovering more starfish, then an entire trove of them all lying together on the ocean floor.

As I swim above them, my shadow crosses over their bodies. A few drift along the bottom, as if trying to get back into the sun.

Absolute paradise.

I break the surface to get my bearings and am surprised to see how far I've come. I can't see the beach or the dock or the employees on their kayaks. Palm trees have sprouted over the cliff that juts into the water.

This area is sandy again, so I walk to the shore. I can follow it back around.

But this is nice. More private than simply sitting away from the others, in full view of how I've set myself apart. It felt fine when Caleb and Sarah joined me, but with them gone, it felt elitist. Anti-social. So not me.

Besides, this little trek is good for sobering up.

Rather than turn back, I keep going. I have hours before we have to return to the ship. My time might be best spent exploring.

The seaweed has been pushed onto the shore in a smooth line, left alone since there was no need to rake it away to place lounge chairs. Sand dollars and sea shells dot the dimpled sand.

But then I spot a set of footprints.

Someone else has walked this way, someone with small feet. Today? Or from some other cruise?

Curious, I shield my hand and stare down the beach.

I spot someone, a small figure kneeling on the shore, building a rather impressively sized structure out of sand.

The glare off the water makes it hard for me to make out who it might be, and an oversized sun hat obscures her features. It's definitely a woman. She wears a black bikini, and a wad of red-flowered fabric tops a straw bag.

I hesitate, trying to decide if I should press forward or go back. The beach stretches beyond her, quiet and unbroken. I can pass her and keep going with only a vague hello.

Her being there settles me, somehow, as if I've met a

kindred spirit who sees the value in taking a moment to absorb the beauty and solitude of this place.

I keep going. I can either walk to the water and skirt her that way, or I can go farther up the beach, where it fades into the scrub brush.

The water is a safer path, as the beach line is littered with natural sea debris, broken limbs, clumps of kelp, and potentially a beached jellyfish or two.

I decide to go with the water.

To avoid disturbing her, I keep my gaze on the horizon, noting the position of the sun. It's high afternoon. I've come far enough around the small island that I can't even see the yacht. The water is unbroken.

I sense that I'm getting close to her. She has to be an employee or the wife of one, so there's no getting out of saying hello. Surely, though, if she's this far afield, she'll also want to keep any pleasantries short.

But before I turn to look at her, I hear a startled gasp.

Concerned she's uncovered a crab or some other unexpected creature in her sand sculpting, I whip around, ready to help.

But she's standing, the breeze ruffling her distinctive brown hair with purple highlights. She holds her hat down, frantically trying to tuck her hair into it.

I'd know that dye job anywhere. Even with the big sunglasses, I recognize her chin, her cheekbones, the line of her jaw. Those small ears. Her shoulders.

I've never seen her with so little on, and I can barely catch my breath. She's like a mirage in the desert, beautiful, perfect.

But this isn't some vision.

It's real.

It's Bailey Johansson. My former assistant. The woman I fired.

The thorn in my side. The problem I have yet to solve.

And she is not supposed to be here.

She sucks in a breath. We're only twenty feet apart.

I swear the ocean sizzles around my feet as my rage builds.

She is *not* supposed to be on this island.

I got rid of her.

Bailey holds out a hand as if to ward me off. "Rhett, don't blow your stack."

But that's exactly what I do.

13

BAILEY

The roar of the ocean is a suitable backdrop as Rhett stalks toward me. It's powerful and loud, and the waves race up the shore like they are staging an attack.

His voice cuts through the noise. "What the fuck are you doing here, Bailey Johansson? This is fraud. This is a fucking crime. I could have you arrested. Didn't you cost this company enough money already?"

Oooh. Dang. Boss man can cuss. I've never heard him do it before.

I consider interrupting to call him out on his language around a lady, but then I decide A: I'm not one, and B: I don't care. The way to rile him is to stay calm and do my thing. It's how I managed working for him.

Still, the F-bombs. That's new.

I tune him out and kneel before my sand sculpture. I kind of enjoy the spectacle. Rhett is in fine wet form, his neck bulging with the effort of being heard over the ocean. Water trickles down a seriously honed chest and muscular arms. If the rest of the employees, especially Viola, could see him, they'd be tattooing "Mr. Juicy" on their bodies.

His green-blue swim trunks cling to him. Dark hair swirls on his legs, wet and sticking to his skin. His dirty feet are covered in sand. They're good-looking feet, not that I have a fetish. Okay, maybe a small one. I do judge a man by his toes.

These are good toes.

And wasted on him, since he's otherwise completely intolerable. His face is beet-red, and the tirade continues. He hasn't come any closer, so I don't feel physically threatened. I smooth the side wall of my structure, still not sure where it's going. I've only been forming a base shape.

His yelling melts into the roar of the waves as I consider the packed sand. There's a moment in sculpting when your design becomes clear. You might start with a standard castle, squared off, towers higher than the wall. But then something happens. Maybe a portion collapses because you didn't get the consistency quite right. Or sometimes the light simply hits it a certain way, and this ignites a new vision.

But this moment, with Rhett's words spitting through the air like an angry cartoon, is when I see what my sculpture will become. It's a sturdy fortress, stalwart against the storm. It reminds me of a mission I saw once on a road trip with my parents.

All the missions in Florida are long gone, but we took a three-day road trip to San Antonio, where tons of historical buildings are still standing. In fact, one was getting decked out to be the backdrop for a wedding while we were there.

A rounded dome of sand brings to mind the Mission San Jose, which had an intact church and a gorgeous line of arches where the light played with shadow. A photographer captured images of a teen girl in a wildly elaborate quinceañera gown while we were there, and I was completely enchanted by how magical it all looked.

While Rhett carries on, I smooth the rounded top and flatten the walls. Then I set to carving out the long row of arches. I can't quite remember what the guide said they once housed. Barracks, maybe?

A shadow crosses my work. He's moved.

Fine.

I peer up. He's quiet, although his face and neck are still red.

"You done?" I ask.

He draws in a deep breath.

Great, another spiel.

I return to my work.

I half expect him to kick the sand, but apparently, he has some restraint. I've almost finished forming the first arch when he kneels next to me and nudges my arm.

"Are you listening to a word I'm saying?"

These words make it through, given they're so close to me.

I sigh. "Not really. Everyone's been on infinite repeat since I got to the island. Bailey, you can't be here. Bailey, you'll get arrested. Bailey, I'm gonna tell Daddy Rhett!"

Oooh, Daddy Rhett. That sends a zip up my spine.

Probably only because he's next to me, half-naked and wet.

"Bailey, what has gotten into you? You can't do things like this."

All right, I'm ready to talk. I face him.

"What has gotten into me? What got into you, Rhett Armstrong, firing me within hours of whatever bullshit Viola handed you, sending me out with security like I haven't been your faithful sidekick for two damn years? Did you need a fall guy? A patsy? Was I simply an easy target?"

Every vein on his neck stands out. "You made a financial hole so big that I'm still trying to unravel it."

"You don't unravel a hole, Rhett. I can dig a hole, and you can fill it. Or I can weave a web, and you can unravel that."

"This is not the time to correct me."

Damn it, he's spoiling my sand time. I want to work on my mission. "Right, because you're the mediocre white man, and you're always right."

This shuts him right up.

I slide my smoothing tool along the curve of the arch, letting the action soothe my frayed nerves. "Yeah, stew on that a minute. Or don't. Because I have a mission to sculpt. Gloria suggested I take some time to myself while she told you I was here."

"She didn't."

"That's obvious. You came out of the sea like a pissed off King Triton ready to attack Ursula."

"I couldn't believe what I was seeing."

I slam the smoothing stick into the sand, burying it

to the hilt. "Welcome to my world, Rhett Armstrong, where after two years of putting up with the likes of you, I get fired for something I had almost nothing to do with!"

"I'm supposed to believe that? You brought me all those requisitions, explaining how marketing was ramping up the budget to acquire new accounts, and it was all a sham!"

"You act as if I know every detail of every company we work with! I bring you all sorts of budgets. I don't make sure the insurance company actually covers us. I bring you the bill. I don't follow the night cleaners around to ensure they work eight hours. We pay them based on a timesheet."

"Well, maybe you should have been more thorough."

"I told you the company was growing faster than you were staffing it. I told you we needed more department-specific oversight."

"I hired a VP of operations."

"Which was great. But we need one over marketing. And finance. You and I were basically the only checks and balances. And we sucked at it."

His chest rises and falls in rapid breaths. "I've been with Dougherty since day one."

"And you need help. But you're too damn stubborn or stupid." I'm done with this conversation. I jerk my smoothing stick out of the ground. It spits a column of sand right in Rhett's face. I have to bite my lip to avoid laughing as Rhett tries to wipe it away, but it sticks to his ocean-salty skin.

I turn my back on him and set to work on the second arch, then the third. I take care not to look his way. I don't know what he's thinking, and I'm not sure I care. I didn't come here for absolution from him.

Okay, maybe I did. Obviously, it's not coming.

Another shadow crosses my mission, but this time it's a heavy cloud. The temperature drops a notch. It's blissful. I need to take a quick dip in the ocean to cool off after working so long in the sun.

But I don't trust Rhett with my sculpture. I've made good headway, and I'm not convinced he won't damage it.

The sun returns. I'm thirsty, so I pull a bottle of water out of my bag. I'd rather be drinking a margarita, but I only got the one, plus a single plate of tacos, before I took off to build a castle. I didn't want to risk being too close during Gloria's reveal to Rhett.

Which she apparently didn't get to. I wonder what that was about.

I finish the third arch and rock back on my heels to assess. I pluck my phone out of my bag. Sometimes the camera sees things my brain fixes when looking with my eyes. And sure enough, as I snap the shot, I realize the dome is too small in proportion with the arches.

Rhett stands, casting a long shadow over my work. "So, that's it?"

I have no answer for him and calmly collect more sand for the dome.

"What am I going to do about you?"

Sigh. He won't shut up. "Pretend I don't exist. Then we'll be the same."

He trudges a few yards away, then stops. I keep him in the corner of my eye as I carefully pack more sand and smooth it down.

Now for details. I want something nostalgic, like maybe a broken-down cart. I don't think I have time to do horses, and I'm not confident I could do animals justice with no access to the Internet for reference material.

Rhett hasn't moved. His arms are crossed, his foot tapping.

I pile up a mound of sand, packing it firmly so I can carve out details. My flat scraper creates clean, smooth lines on all four sides. A strange sound separates itself from the dull roar of the waves. I glance at Rhett. He's talking to himself, complete with hand gestures.

This makes me laugh. Sure, Rhett, give your speech to the palm trees.

Another cloud drifts in, providing blessed relief from the sun. I keep working.

Eventually Rhett takes off walking along the shore.

Is that it? Have I won?

He's not headed back to the party beach unless he's planning to walk the entire circumference of the island. He skulks down the shore with a stiff-legged stride like an angry Frankenstein. He comes to an outcropping of rock that looks impenetrable, so he wades out into the water and dives below the surface.

I stand up, watching. I catch a small glimpse of him as he comes up for a breath. He's swimming around the rocks.

Then I can't see him.

He's gone!

The cloud cover continues, and a stronger breeze kicks up, cooling me down. This is nice. I'll walk back for another margarita in a minute. If Rhett is going to circle the entire island, I have time for booze and tacos before he makes it back.

But for now, I want to carve a perfect wooden cart.

And exult in my success.

Because I don't think Rhett Armstrong has the guts to kick me off the boat.

I laugh out loud. "Got you!" I call into the waves.

But in response, several fat drops of water land on my mission.

No, no!

I peer up at the sky. The clouds have gathered over-head. Is it going to rain on my sculpture?

I work swiftly to finish the cart.

I hollow out the inside as well as I can. The wheels are tricky, particularly at the base, where they want to crumble into the sand.

A light sprinkle starts to fall. I shove my phone in my bag so it won't get wet, then immediately dig it out again to take a picture. I can feel bigger drops on my back, and I bet it's about to come down. Nobody mentioned rain when we boated out to the island, but then I showed up really late. Maybe everyone else was given a heads-up.

I snap close-ups, a broader shot, then get on my belly to take an image with the gorgeous unbroken water behind it. I'm glad I walked a good distance so that I don't have the cruise ship in the background.

But then, unexpectedly, I *do* have the ship in my shot.

Why has the ship moved? Shouldn't it stay in place until the small boats go back? Doesn't it have an anchor the size of a small town holding it in place?

Panic rises. What is going on?

Then the deluge hits. It rains so hard that it feels like needles on my skin.

I toss everything in my bag and start racing toward the main beach.

14

———

RHETT

When I emerge from the water after another lengthy swim around a rock outcropping, I realize it's raining.

Nobody mentioned anything about a storm today. Surely I would have been briefed if there were any threats that might cut the day short.

I pause, trying to decide if I should go back the way I came, which is a known distance, or press on.

I scan the beach ahead. It's unbroken for quite a while, but there's no hint of the party beach. And I can't see the ship either, so there's a lot of curving around to do.

Bailey is on the way back. I should go that way. Make sure she's not working on that castle, ignoring the change in weather.

I dive back into the water, reversing my path like a real-life version of "Going on a Bear Hunt," a song we would sing at camp when I was a kid.

I'm coming to a rock.

Can't go over it.
Can't go under it.
Have to swim around it.

When I make it back to the secondary beach, I take off in a solidly paced run, sticking to the packed wet sand to avoid the slowdown of the water or the potential pitfalls of debris farther up the shore.

It's not long before I make it to the soggy mounds that used to be Bailey's castle. She isn't here.

Good. She's probably back to the safety of the group.

I pause for a moment, shielding my eyes from the rain. The ocean is an enormous bank of gray, the water pelting its surface. There is no longer any distinction between the waves and the horizon.

Rather than swim around this last outcropping, I head to the trees where I originally saw the sand foot-prints emerge. There's nothing now. The rain has washed away all evidence of Bailey's path. But I'd rather stay on land at this point, and the trees will provide some protection.

There's a sandy trail that I follow. I push my hair out of my eyes. Hell of a thing, getting caught in a storm like this, alone on an island. As mad as I am at Bailey for what she's done, I hope she wasn't afraid.

I emerge from the trees, realizing it's quite a way to the huts. I forgot that I swam the distance the first time. But I think I can make out the buildings in the rain.

I push off for another run. The rain gets heavier, stinging my face.

I haven't gone very far when I nearly trip over a lounger. There's three sitting together.

This was mine, where I sat with Caleb and Sarah.

My soggy towel, shirt, and shoes are on the ground, almost hidden beneath it.

I snatch them up and keep going. I should make it to the main grouping of chairs any minute.

I curse when my knee hits another lounger, then another. I'm in the middle of them. They're hard to discern in the driving rain. I'm not sure how we're even going to take the boat back to the ship. Maybe every-one's waiting it out in the hut.

But something tells me I'm wrong. I know the hut isn't big enough for our entire group. And the kayak hut isn't either.

I spot the brown structure ahead. Thank God. It doesn't have doors, just an open side.

I lunge across the threshold and pause, panting from the exertion of the swim and the lengthy run.

There's no one here.

Everything was clearly packed in a hurry. There are bags of trash lining one wall. The table hasn't been wiped down. The big hand-crank ice crusher sits forlornly on the metal stand on the opposite side, the oversized bowl beneath it. There's even ice floating in the bottom on an inch of water.

Lightning cracks, and I turn to look over the ocean, or where it ought to be. There's nothing but gray, briefly lit up in the flash. I think I see the ship in the distance, but I'm not sure.

Is there some emergency bunker here I don't know about? Could everyone be in it?

I head to the bowl of ice and scoop a handful of water in my mouth. At least I'm no longer salty from my run in the rain.

I refuse to panic. Surely they couldn't have gotten everyone back on the boat while I was walking around the island. How long has it been?

I lift my wrist and tap my waterproof watch.

I was gone for over two hours.

Well, that *is* enough time.

I survey the hut. There's a kitchen area in the back where staff assembled the oyster platters and replenished the taco fixings from coolers. It's a rudimentary setup with no appliances. But there is a sink on the back counter.

The counters are all empty.

Damn it. Obviously, the captain realized a storm was coming, or had unexpectedly turned toward this island, and called everyone back early. Nobody noticed my things so far away. With two boats, it was probably easy to assume that someone you don't see is on the other one. We hadn't exactly assigned buddies.

Lighting cracks again. I step to the edge of the hut, peering at the dock. I can barely make out the long walkway.

There is no movement, not anywhere. Another flash confirms my suspicion. The dock is empty. Both the passenger and the crew boats are gone.

I don't know how long it will take for anyone to notice I'm not there. I'm rooming alone. I scared Gloria off. If I don't answer my door, they'll assume I'm trying to work.

Great. Just great.

The wind shifts directions suddenly, pelting me with rain. The branches of the high palm trees swirl madly.

I step farther back into the hut. I'll simply have to wait this out.

I wring out my towel and shirt and lay them over the table. I drop my sodden shoes to the ground. At least this hut seems sturdy.

I walk to the cabinets in the back. Maybe the crew left something behind to eat. I'm ravenous after all the exercise. I step behind the counter in hopes of a forgotten cooler, and I see a huddled ball in the back. Another bag of trash? It's not black, but grayish-white with blotches of red.

Another peal of thunder cracks, and I take a step forward as the light flashes in the shadows.

It's definitely not garbage.

It's Bailey, and she's crying her eyes out.

15

BAILEY

This isn't happening.

It can't be.

No, no, no, no.

The floor is hard beneath my soaked body. My cover-up clings to me like wet tissue. I'm cold, somehow, even though the air is muggy. I'm leaning against a rough, unfinished cabinet, and I might have a splinter in my cheek.

But worst of all, everyone left me.

Bailey Johansson, the colossal fraud who sneaked onto the boat, is getting her due. She's alone in a storm on an island with no electricity, no cell signal, no way to contact anyone to come back for her.

I picture myself trying to be Tom Hanks in *Castaway*, befriending a—well, there's not even a volleyball here. A kayak? A coconut? Are there coconuts here? Could I *eat* the coconut if it became my friend?

A tremendous gust of wind rattles the shack, and I can't help it. I scream.

It feels good, so I scream again at the top of my lungs, like I'm the wind itself.

Then arms are around me. Strong, comforting arms. They lift me off the floor like I'm nothing.

I think this is it. The hut came tumbling down, and I'm dead. This is Jesus, or an angel, or my long-gone grandma here to fetch me for the afterlife. I've become light as a feather, my dumb ol' body gone.

But then a flash of lightning reveals the truth.

It's the devil, and I'm on my way to hell.

Rhett Armstrong.

I kick and twist to get away from him. "Let me down!"

His grip gets tighter, so I lean close to his ear and scream as loud as I did when I thought I was alone.

He drops me like a hot skillet.

I stumble, grabbing at the counter to avoid falling. Then I'm up and standing and reaching on tiptoes to get in his face. "What the hell happened?"

The wind rattles the building again, but I'm too mad to scream.

Rhett shakes his head. "I don't know. I got here after you."

I pound my fists on his chest. "They left us! We were fighting, and they left us! This is your fault for yelling at me for half an hour!"

"You would have been off making your castle even if I hadn't come along."

He's right. I stop pounding and step away.

"Wasn't there a list?" My voice is so high-pitched

that I barely recognize it. "Shouldn't they have checked it twice, like Santa Claus? Like kindergarten?"

"They didn't seem to track who got on the boat on the way here." Rhett slicks his wet hair back where it's fallen in his eyes. He's shirtless and shoeless, and there are those toes again.

I walk a few steps away. "You'd think they'd scan us or check us off or something."

"It's a private cruise." He leans on the counter, staring out at the rain. A lounger tumbles past. "This is a big storm."

My stomach clenches. "It's not a hurricane, is it?"

He shakes his head, sending rivulets down his temples. He brushes them away. "They can't build that fast. We would have known if one was coming."

"Did you even look? Did the captain?"

"I'm sure."

I move next to him, tapping his arm. Dang, it's like a steel beam. "But you don't know that, do you? Is it possible that some cocky ship captain, perhaps descended from some other cocky ship captain who steered at high speeds through icebergs, didn't want to lose a high-paying gig?"

"It's his neck on the line, too."

"Yeah, I don't think the captain of the Titanic thought of that either."

Rhett has no retort. An eerie creaking sound makes him look up at the roof of the hut.

My anger sizzles into fear. "Are we safe here?"

"I'm not sure." He heads to the open side to peer out.

I don't follow him. It's pointless. The rain is a sheet of gray. The only thing we can see is the occasional passing by of a chair or a bush that has blown loose from the ground.

There's a crash outside to the left.

I return to the corner of the cabinets and curl back into my ball. I'm going to die, and it's going to be with Rhett Armstrong!

Long moments pass. There's a screeching of metal and more crashing. I crawl to the end of the counter and look around it. Rhett isn't there!

Am I alone? Did he get swept out to sea?

But then he's back, dripping, shaking water off his arms.

I stand up. "What's happening?"

"It's the racks for the kayaks and the life jackets. They've blown over. The dock is fine."

I didn't think of that. If the dock goes, can they even come pick us up?

I feel sick. I lean over the counter, groaning.

"Are you all right?" Rhett asks.

"No."

"What's wrong?"

I peer at him in the gloom. "What's wrong? I'm stranded on a private island. There's a terrible storm. And I'm with —" I don't know what to call him. Evil incarnate? The biggest dick in America? My arch nemesis? "YOU!"

"We're going to be fine, Bailey. Someone will realize we're gone. They'll know where we are. You can probably sue them for mental anguish and add another payday to your last one."

I whip my head around. "My last one? What? My last check from your office? I didn't exactly get severance. I noticed you had HR calculate it to literally the minute I was escorted out."

His gaze bores into mine. "I mean, for whatever marketing sham you set up. What did you spend that half a mil on, Bailey? Maxwell?"

What is he talking about? "Maxwell isn't that expensive."

Well, other than that pricey kitty litter.

But that leads to another thought. My sweet cat! If I die, I hope my pet sitter adopts him!

Rhett shakes his head. "Right."

"What would you know about Maxwell? You don't even know that I had nothing to do with that marketing snafu other than to bring you the requisitions."

His eyebrows draw together. "Oh, really?"

We're back to that. It never ends. What was I thinking, coming on this trip, hoping I would be heard?

And look at me. I'm going to die on this island, and my last words will be to this idiotic man!

Another metallic screech makes us both look out through the opening of the hut. It's easy to imagine the entire building collapsing.

Rhett holds up his hands. "We will table this discussion until we're back on the ship. For now, we have to ride out this storm. Even if they realize we're gone, they can't safely come back for us right now."

He's right.

I rest my head on the counter. Ouch. Another splinter. I poke my temple to make sure nothing's lodged in my skin.

A kayak skims by the hut, sliding along the wet sand like it's water. It reminds me of the scene in the *Wizard of Oz* when Dorothy sees the mean lady riding through the air on her bicycle.

A ripping sound draws our attention to the ceiling. A corner of the thatched roof peels back like a giant invisible hand opening a tin can.

Rain pours into the hut, splattering all over the ice crusher and knocking over the bowl.

Rhett and I both step back against the far counter.

More of the top tears away, and the wild lash of rain reaches us.

"What do we do?" I call out to him, trying to hang onto my whipping hair.

He opens a cabinet. "These are bolted to the cement. Crawl in."

I hesitate. The space is small. But then the rest of the roof gives way, and the walls shudder. We're instantly drenched.

I dive inside and curl up in the far back. There are a few supplies down here, but it's too dark to see what they are. I push them out of my way.

Rhett crawls in the opposite side and closes the door. "We'll be safe from flying debris."

"What if these tear away from the floor?" My fear is so intense that my whole body shudders. I'm not sure I want to hear the answer.

When his low voice rumbles in the dark space, it's not reassuring.

"If that happens, we're done for."

16

RHETT

This is one hell of a situation.

We can hear the hut dismantling around us. I'm grateful for a concrete floor and hefty, well-anchored cabinets.

But even so, these won't withstand an intense tropical storm.

Bailey's crying again, huddled in the corner. I don't know what made me want to comfort her the first time, but I'm not going to try it again. She's as prickly as a briar patch and about as welcoming.

It's not easy to fold myself up into a small enough package to hunker down in the cabinets. At least she's a better size for it.

My elbow bumps into a cardboard box. Maybe they leave a few supplies between trips.

Of course. The cruise line comes here often. Even if they don't notice we're gone, they'll be back with another round of visitors, eventually. With the storm, though, they'll probably skirt the area or reschedule for a day or two.

Bailey sniffs. "What's whirring inside that evil mind?"

I swallow a salty reply. "Nothing." Of course, Bailey thinks I'm evil. I fired her. I was not a friendly boss. She's right about what she said earlier. We were in over our heads, and we didn't have an easy time of it in the office.

Half of it was my fault, deciding I had to be a certain type of leader. Some of it was Uncle Sherman's. Holding a secret that large made it hard to get overly friendly with anyone, lest they be upset later that I with-held information that important about the company.

But some of it was because of Bailey. She wanted my office to run her way. Her filing system. Her spread-sheets. Her organization. We were bound to butt heads.

"Still calculating what I owe your damn company?" Bailey shifts in the dark, her foot brushing my ankle.

"Just listening to the storm."

"Oh."

Now I do actually listen. The screech of metal has ended, but rain drums on the top of the counter. It leaks in the corners and around the doors, but we're wet anyway, so it doesn't matter.

It's eerie and strange, curled in the dark with Bailey. After a while, she quits trying to avoid bumping me, and our legs rest against each other. I lean against the box behind me, bracing my head on the soggy top.

When might we be missed? There's a dinner tonight,

but I have been eating in my room, so my absence might not be questioned. And even if Gloria knocks on my door, there are a dozen reasons why I might not answer. I could be in the pool, or at the bar, or simply ignoring it to work. She wouldn't exactly ask the crew to open my door.

How long might that go on? There was nothing highlighted on the itinerary for the port tomorrow that required my presence. After that stop, it's the last night of the trip.

It might not be until the cleaning staff finds my things in the room when the cruise is over that they realize something is amiss.

"Do you think anyone will report you missing?" I ask Bailey.

"I wasn't even supposed to be on the ship."

"What about Viola?"

"She's super mad at me."

"But you were such great friends."

"And then she got me fired."

This statement shakes me to the core. "What do you mean, she *got* you fired? You two were clearly very tight. She was upset when she brought those requisitions in."

Bailey blows out a long gust of air that tickles my knees. "I am not one to question the ways of Viola. It was impossible to talk to her today."

"What did she say?"

"The same thing everyone else did. 'Why are you here? You were *fired*, Bailey.'" Her voice is a sneer.

"So she won't report you as missing."

Bailey sighs. "I don't have a roommate in the cabin."

"Me either."

"Gloria from HR might look for me. She really didn't tell you I was here? She was the one who suggested I find a quiet spot while she told you."

I hazily recollect Gloria approaching our chairs during the alcohol-infused portion of the afternoon. "It may not have been a good time for such a bit of news."

"What's that supposed to mean?"

"I was drinking with Sarah and her husband."

"You drink?"

"I'm not the boss all the time."

"But that suggests you have *fun*."

"There are quite a few people in this world who think I should be *more* serious."

She shifts suddenly, and there's a *bonk* sound. "Owww. Dang it. Rhett Armstrong, don't say such crazy things when I'm in a small space."

I keep my chuckle to myself. "You okay? We don't need a head injury adding to our woes here."

"I'm fine. And if you got any more serious, you'd be brain surgery."

I see no reason to enlighten her about my life or my decisions. "The rain has lessened."

"You going to check things out?"

"I should."

"How long do you think we'll be stuck here?"

I glance at my watch. It's already late afternoon. "Unless someone reports us, *and* they think we're in danger, *and* the storm has cleared the area, I'm guessing we're stuck here for at least a night."

"A night?"

"And that's only if they turned the ship around. If

they kept going to Freeport, then they're too far to simply return. Someone will have to come from Florida."

"But it took a day and a night to get *here*!"

"Exactly. So it's most likely we'll be discovered when the company returns to this location with another ship."

"When might that happen?"

"Hard to say."

She makes another sudden movement, and her head bonks the counter again. "Dang it!"

"We'll be okay. There's water."

"But the signs say not to drink it!"

Oh, so it's non-potable ocean water. I hadn't looked, sitting far from the huts. "We'll figure out a way to make it safe."

Her voice goes higher in pitch. "But we don't have a fire to boil it."

"Bailey, we'll figure it out. Let me look outside."

She sniffles. I hesitate, wondering if I should say something comforting, but instead, I push on the cabinet door.

It doesn't want to open, and I realize there are tree limbs and debris blocking it. I shove hard, and the door swings widely enough for me to crawl out.

The hut is a disaster. Everything is wet and muddy. There's all manner of junk filling the space. Life jackets. Branches. Opened trash bags.

I wish I had brought my shoes in with me.

The rain is coming down, but nothing like before. I pick my way around the counter.

The hut is more or less intact, other than the roof, which is completely gone.

The hand-crank margarita machine is bolted down near the side wall. The colorful rainbow skirt attached to the edges of the metal stand is a sodden mess.

The table where the oysters sat on trays is on its side, and luckily enough, this trapped my sandals in place. I tug them out, muddy and wet, but at least I won't step on anything that could cut my feet.

I move to the open side, my gut twisting at what I see.

Kayaks are strewn all over the beach, the metal racks that held them mangled and dismantled. Lounge chairs are everywhere—in the water, upturned on the sand, scattered in the tree line.

The hut that housed the bathrooms has totally collapsed. The bamboo roof that was so cleverly decorative a few hours ago lies on top of the rubble like pickup sticks. Thank goodness we didn't shelter in there.

I walk to the other side, where the kayak racks were before they got tossed around. The equipment shed is intact, including its roof. It was smaller, and possibly more sturdily built.

But the worst part is the dock.

The end is twisted, probably by the force of the waves, leaving jagged metal jutting out. The wood planks splintered away like broken spaghetti.

There's no way to pull up a motorized boat now. The water is too shallow, and the dock is unusable.

The cruise line will have to first know that there is a problem, and if they don't realize we're here, they might simply shuttle all their island stops elsewhere without sending someone in a rowboat to reach the shore. They might not even have a rowboat on board.

And if they act like most companies, they will wait on budgets, subcontractor estimates, and a cleanup crew before they make actual landfall and figure out we're here.

Bailey and I might be stuck here for days.

17

BAILEY

I'm not just soaked but filthy.

Rhett took too long, so finally I pushed open my cabinet door to tumble out onto a pile of muddy tree branches.

I grimace at my white cover-up. It's clinging to my black suit, and now one side is brown. I peer up at the open sky where the roof used to be. The rain is coming down, but nothing like it was.

I tug the wrap into place as best I can and shove my hair out of my face. I don't know when I lost my hair tie, and unless I dig out my bag from this mess, I'm not going to be able to pull it back with my spare.

I'm grateful for my flip-flops as I pick my way around the counter to the main opening of the hut. It's remarkably intact, other than the roof, although the floor has standing water and one of the tables has been overturned.

I approach the open side and spot Rhett immediately, still shirtless, standing in the rain and peering out over the dock.

Or what used to be a dock.

This can't be good.

I walk up to him, hoping the rain will wash off the mud. "That looks bad."

"It is. They'll have to use a shallow boat that can get to us. Maybe they can anchor the tender as close as possible, and we can swim out."

"I can swim."

"You might have to." He glances down at my feet. "Good, you have shoes. There's a lot of sharp debris around."

I survey the landscape. The bathroom hut is a pile of broken bamboo. Great. I'm going to have to pee in the trees. But then I see the other building. "Hey, the kayak shed has a roof. Have you checked it out?"

"Not yet."

The two of us tromp over, sinking in the wet sand and skirting the random kayaks lying around. The doors are thrown wide.

We step inside, and it's bliss to be out of the rain for a moment. It's mostly empty, the space kept open to roll the racks back in between visits.

"They must have left in a hurry to leave all this out," I say.

Rhett grunts.

On the back wall, there's a counter with supplies and tools, presumably to work on equipment that needs repair. Rhett moves toward it. "There's a toolbox," he says. "That might come in handy."

For what, I don't know, but I guess it means we're one step evolved from smashing coconuts on rocks.

More life jackets, many of them faded, are piled in a corner. But they're dry.

"We can sleep on those, I guess, if we have to," Rhett says.

I look at the pile with doubt. "I think I'd rather pull a lounge chair in here, if we can find any unbroken ones."

"Now that's a good idea," he says.

I resent the rush of good feelings that come over me when he says it. I don't want to associate him with anything but bull-headed ignorance.

"I'll go start looking." It's as good an excuse as any to get away from him.

I regret my choice almost instantly when the rain pelts me again. It's a lot cooler than it was before the storm, and I've been wet for what feels like days.

But I spot a contender—a lounger folded up in the sand. I approach it and work to tug it open.

No dice. It's missing half of the middle section.

The next three are similarly useless, but then I find one almost wholly intact, only a few of the stretchy bands holding it to the frame unraveled.

I fold it up and start lugging it back to the equipment shed.

Rhett is still there, arranging tools on the counter.

I shake my head at him. I'm thirsty, hungry, and wrung out from stress, and he's sorting screwdrivers. I unfold my lounger and plop onto the seat, ready for a rest.

But the moment my weight hits the canvas surface, the bands quickly unwind from the frame.

My butt hits the floor as I fall straight through with an "oof."

Rhett turns around, and I don't need to see his smirk to know it's there.

My feet are in the air, my body folded in half like a taco. My arms are trapped on either side of my body, shoulders wedged against the frame.

I wiggle and shift, trying to get out, but I only seem to get more stuck.

Now Rhett can't control himself, and his barely suppressed chuckle fills the space.

Oh, so *now* the stern boss man learns to laugh.

He approaches. "Need a hand?"

"No." I stubbornly twist from side to side, trying to work my arms free so I can lift myself out of this mess.

He stands over me, watching me struggle. "Bailey, let me help."

"No. I've got this."

I decide down is better than up, and scoot my butt backward in hopes of getting a leg free.

Only now I'm folded up beneath the frame, and my ankles are caught on the bottom rung.

I close my eyes. This is too much.

A squeaky sound makes me look. Rhett is using a ratchet to loosen a bolt on the side. Suddenly, the frame breaks apart, and I'm flat on the ground.

Thank God.

I roll away from the canvas-and-metal death trap

and stand up. The life jackets are starting to look better as a cushion.

I'm about to head for them to make a bed-pile, when Rhett holds out his arm. "Hey, hold up. You're hurt."

He takes my elbow and pulls me close. "You got cut by the chair."

I glance down. A line of red has welled up on my upper arm.

"I'll live."

"Let's not chance it. Not out here."

He leads me back into the rain. The wetness stings the cut.

"Where are we going? There's not exactly an urgent care down the block."

"At least wash it off in the sink. It's fed by rainwater. I spotted the collection tank that feeds into the main hut."

I hold my hand up to the sky. "We have plenty of rainwater!"

Still, I follow him to the roofless building. He picks up the "Welcome, Blue Sapphire guests" sign that was strung over the entry but has fallen onto the wet sand.

He ties it to the back corner, then rehangs it sideways over the protected space made by the counters. When he's done, we have a decent tarp protecting us from the rain in the most secure part of the hut.

I admit, I'm impressed.

He shoves aside branches and kneels before the cabinet he sat in during the storm. "Time to assess what we've got here. Maybe there will be some paper towels or something."

He pulls out a box, which turns out to be packets of margarita mix that the woman used to flavor the slush. I pick one up. It's liquid inside and already has tequila measured into it.

"Score!" I say, holding it close like a prized possession.

Rhett dives back down, returning with a large yellow bucket. He sets it on the counter and turns it around to read the label. "Dill pickles in brine."

"Crack that baby open. I'm hungry."

"Don't take in too much salt. We don't have water."

"Spoilsport."

He reaches around inside the cabinet and returns triumphantly with what looks like a red tackle box, the kind my dad used for his lures when fishing off the docks.

It has a big white cross on it. "First aid kit?" I ask.

"I bet so." He unlatches the front, careful to slide it beneath the most protected part of the tarp.

Inside are bandages, peroxide, gauze, Q-Tips, antibiotic packets, adhesive tape, and the cold packs you shake to activate.

"Let's take this to the shed, and we'll get you treated. You don't want to get an infection out here." Rhett's eyes meet mine. "Okay?"

This hesitancy gives me pause. He's not ordering me now. He's hoping I'll go along.

"Okay, sure." I look lovingly at my pickle bucket. "Can we bring that?"

"Sure." Rhett snaps the kit closed and carries it in one hand, and the handle of the pickle bucket in the other.

I reluctantly leave my margarita packet on the counter. "I'll be back," I whisper.

The rain washes the blood off my arm and most of the mud off my cover-up. We duck through the shed doors and sit on the floor.

Rhett unrolls a length of gauze. My cut is too long for Band-Aids.

I guess he's doing this. It's my right arm, so I doubt I could manage with my left, anyway.

I brace my elbow on my prized pickle bucket.

"This might sting." He squeezes a packet of antibiotic ointment down the cut, then covers it with the gauze.

Fire licks across my skin. "Yowsa!" I cry out.

"Sorry," he says.

His fingers are gentle as he holds the gauze in place and tears off a length of tape with his teeth.

They're good teeth, too, long and straight and white. For a moment, I have a startling vision of him biting the inside of my wrist. It's one of my weaknesses. I think it comes from all my teen years of watching Gomez kissing Morticia on *The Addams Family* followed too quickly by vampire shows.

I *love* vampire shows.

I immediately push that thought away. This is Rhett we're talking about. Evil incarnate.

He's neatly surrounded the gauze with a double line

of tape. "That should hold," he says. "I guess we'll have to be careful around those loungers."

I pull my arm away from him, afraid that my body might betray my unexpected yearning to be the Bella to his Edward. "Yeah, we will."

He points out the open door. "Rain is finally letting up."

Huh. He's right. The storm is passing.

He stands up, and every muscle works in perfect coordination as he reaches his full height. I hug my pickle bucket. I can't think of anything useful to say, so I blurt, "Can we make pickle margaritas now? We can mix the packets with the pickle water."

His mouth flirts with a smile. "That wise?"

"What else are we going to do here? Make a tree-house and play Tarzan?"

"That's a jungle, and this is—"

"Shut up, Rhett. I know it's an island."

"I know you know. I'm teasing you."

Rhett Armstrong, teasing? That's new.

He doesn't even complain when we have to lug the pickle bucket back to the hut. The clouds part as we make our way across the sand, and by the time I'm ripping open the first margarita packet with my teeth, the sun is actually shining.

18

RHETT

When we return to the food hut, Bailey and I make an amazing discovery. Beneath the metal stand holding the hand-crank ice crusher, there's a cooler!

I drag it out and we bend over it, grinning at each other as I flip the top.

It's full of oysters! And bagged ice!

"We're saved!" Bailey cries, and her arms go around my neck.

For a moment, my vision narrows. There's nothing here but her, the damp cover-up, her hair tickling my jaw. She's against me, the gauze on her skin brushing my arm. She smells of shampoo and rain.

So, this is how it could be. If we weren't boss and assistant turned adversaries. Part of a colossal corporate disaster.

This is Bailey operating in normal mode.

Then she catches herself and pulls away. "Sorry. I get excited over food."

I have to laugh. "You can hate me and still be excited about ice and oysters."

"Good," she says. "Because I am. And I do."

But even though she's confirming our animosity, there's no bite to her words. Hopefully, we can avoid all talk of our work history and be amicable while we wait for someone to notice we're here.

Because, technically, I'm not her boss.

This isn't work.

I pull out the first tray of oysters, their pearly shells glistening below the plastic cover. There are two more below.

"Did you eat any earlier?" I ask her.

"No. I only had eyes for the tacos."

"But you like them?"

"At this point, I'd eat them raw." She pulls the plastic top off the first tray and lifts a shell to her mouth. "You're supposed to swallow them whole, right?"

I only get out the words, "You can. But they are—" when she tilts her head back and tips the shell in her mouth.

Then her eyes go wide. She presses her free hand to her lips. She shakes her head.

"It's fine to chew them." I don't know if this information is helpful or not, because she walks in a tight circle.

She drops the shell and pleads at me with her eyes.

I'm not sure what to do. We don't have fresh water at the moment, only ice. I pry open the pickle bucket. The large pickles bob in the juice.

She nods vigorously. I think she's still holding the oyster in her mouth.

"You can spit it out."

Her eyes water as she shakes her head for no.

I realize we don't have any cups. I take the oyster shell from her and dip it in the pickle juice. I pass it to her.

She tips it into her mouth, her fingers pressed against the side wall of the hut like she's trying to hang on.

Then, finally, she lets out a breath. "That was awful."

"It's not everyone's favorite. Why didn't you spit it out?"

"I need the food. I have to eat it."

"What was bad about it?"

"It tasted like old seawater!"

I bite my lip. The salty ocean flavor is what most people like. "Did the pickle juice help? There was hot sauce and other options when they had them out earlier."

"It did."

She stares down at the tray of oysters. "I might have to get a lot hungrier before I eat any more of those."

"We can't wait too long. They're raw—"

"They're what?"

"Oysters on a half shell are usually served raw."

She presses both hands to her neck like she's about to choke. "I ate raw food?"

"I take it you're not much on seafood. Didn't you grow up in Florida?"

"I ate burgers and pizza like everybody else!"

I pick up a shell and slurp it back.

"Is it okay? Did they go bad?"

I set the shell next to Bailey's on the table. "They were better with the sauces, but it seems fine."

She squeezes her eyes shut. "Ooooh! This sucks! Why didn't they leave tacos?"

"Fate."

"Oh, just give me a pickle. A big one."

I hold back on every improper response and pluck a pickle from the bucket.

Bailey holds it with both hands. It's a particularly girthy one, and as she opens her mouth to take a bite, I intend to look away. It's too much. Too suggestive.

But my eyes refuse to focus anywhere else. Her pink lips part, showing a flash of teeth. Then she bites down with a crunch.

Okay, I'm able to avert my gaze for that part. I slurp down two more oysters, then set aside the trays for a moment to consider the ice.

It won't last long in this heat. I lift the bag, considering the water pooling at the bottom. We have to drink it without losing any.

"Did you notice any cups in the cabinet you were in? We only checked my side earlier."

Bailey shakes her head, chomping another big bite of pickle. Then she says, "But there were boxes. They might have disposable plates and cups."

I carefully repack everything in the cooler and latch it closed. "We'll want to take care of that water and stay out of the sun. Getting through this is the name of the game."

"Oooh, I know how to desalinate water with plastic bottles," she said. "We did it in seventh grade science."

"Nice idea, but do we have water bottles?"

She frowns. "I have one in my bag." She glances around. "Wherever that is. I think I left it on the floor before we crawled into the cabinets."

"I think we need two, though." I didn't grow up on the seaboard, but I vaguely recall the double-bottle technique from my textbook.

"The cup holding the ocean water doesn't have to be a water bottle," she says. "It just has to fit inside it."

"Right." I remember that now.

"Let's go look. If there's cups, they might collapse enough to push inside the bottom of the water bottle." She frowns, her expression adorable as two lines appear between her arched brows. "But we'll have to cut the bottom off the bottle and fold it in."

"There's shears in the shed."

"Oh. Good then." She pushes the rest of her pickle in her mouth and brushes her hands against each other.

We both head to the brush-laden back of the hut. I cleared the floor around my cabinet, but the corner is filled with debris.

"How did mud get in here?" Bailey asks.

"No idea. It was quite a storm."

We move branches aside to reach the corner cabinet.

"My bag!" Bailey cries, pulling it out from under a palm branch. It's muddy and wet, but she slings it onto a bare spot of the counter.

"My notebook," Bailey says, trying to flatten a bent spiral pad with an illustration of an orange tabby on the cover. At the bottom, the words, "I heart Maxwell" have been sketched in.

Right. Maxwell.

I focus on my work, wishing for gloves as the limbs stab at my skin. I stack them in the back corner as neatly as I can. We might want to build a fire later.

The idea of spending a night on the island brings me pause. I've walked and swum about half the perimeter, but we haven't tried to penetrate the brush of the interior. It's unlikely there is any dangerous wildlife, but there could be snakes or poisonous insects.

Nothing living here will be used to humans invading their nighttime.

"Here's the water bottle," Bailey says, holding up a hefty half-liter bottle, mostly empty. "It's pretty wide, so a cup could easily go inside it if we can find one."

"Didn't we barely get any usable water out of the experiment, though?" My memories of this are hazy.

"Yeah, I feel like it was only a few drops from condensation. But maybe here it will be more? We were inside with air conditioning. And you know, we were kids. We weren't trying to survive."

I nod. I've cleared a path to the corner cabinet, so I pull it open. There's two boxes inside. One says, "Paper cups." The other, "Wood utensils."

I pull out the box of cups.

"Perfect!" Bailey says. "We can modify them and make lots of desalinators!"

I feel dubious about it working. "We can make some.

For now, though, we're all right with the melted ice. We need to stay out of the sun and keep as cool as possible."

Bailey leans on her elbows, watching me stack another pile of branches. "You, Rhett Armstrong, are never cool." She spreads her straw bag out to dry. "And when you're firing someone, you are the least cool of all."

There's no answer to that.

The cup box is half full, and I pluck out a stack. "You thirsty?"

"After the pickled oyster? Totally."

We head back to the cooler. I carefully untie one of the ice bags and pour two cups of water.

Bailey holds hers against her cheek. "I'm so grateful for this."

I take a sip. The water is deliciously cold. "Same."

Bailey watches me over her cup. "Same? Is prickly ol' Rhett using the language of the lesser man?"

"Bailey…"

"The slang of the street? The youth-speak?" At my frown, she laughs, and the sound in the sun with the blue sky above makes me feel like everything isn't completely off the rails. Like we're not stuck on an isolated island with only ice and oysters. Like this is all part of the fun.

She pokes me on the forehead. "It's all there."

"In my brain?"

"No, in those anger lines. There's three of them, straight as arrows, and they show up when you're being a judgmental ogre."

"I'm not judging."

"You are. You're judging me for wanting to desalinate water. For screaming in a storm. For not wanting to play survivor."

"We've been alone for two hours, tops."

"Exactly." She examines the ice crusher. "I think I can work this."

"We have plenty of water. We don't need to crack any ice."

She lifts the metal top of the crusher. "Yes, we do."

"For what?"

She heads to the back counter and collects the margarita packet she took out earlier. "If I'm going to be stuck on an island with you, I most definitely need a *drink*."

19

BAILEY

I want a margarita, and I want it now.

I hold my pre-measured mix like the treasure it is. For a brief, glorious moment, I consider chug-a-lugging the extra-strength flavoring laced with tequila straight from the bag.

But it will be too strong, and I've had enough foul-tasting things for one afternoon.

I realize when I return to the ice crusher that the original bowl is buried in sticks and leaves.

Dang it.

I carefully prop the opened packet against the base of the ice crusher. I retrieve the bowl and run it back to the sink.

I ignore the non-potable water warning sign over the sink, digging branches out of the basin and flinging them aside.

The alcohol will kill any bacteria.

It will. I insist it will.

Miraculously, water runs clear and strong from the

faucet. I realize we don't need to create the desalinators. This is rainwater. Maybe it only says non-potable because it sits here too long and they are extra careful.

We're going to be fine.

I wash out the bowl as best I can. When it is presentable, I return to the ice crusher and dump the packet of tequila mix directly into the bowl. I don't have a big pitcher like the staff used, but I will make do. In fact, I might drink my margarita straight from this bowl.

Rhett watches me warily from where he sits on the cooler.

If he thinks he's going to block my way to the ice with his butt, he better think again.

I slide the bowl underneath the mouth of the ice crusher, careful not to spill a single precious drop of my mix.

Then I cock out a hip, staring Rhett down. "I need the ice."

"Alcohol will get you more dehydrated," he says.

I shove his shoulder. "I said, get your butt off my ice!"

He sighs and stands, walking to the edge of the hut to look out over the debris-laden sand.

"And don't tell me not to spill the water," I shout when he seems like he might be about to say something.

He crosses his arms but continues to face away.

I lift the lid of the cooler, averting my eyes from the trays of oysters. I open a bag and use an extra paper cup to scoop ice out of it. I fill the metal tank of the ice crusher with what I randomly estimate to be the proper amount of ice for the mix. There's a range of strength for margaritas that is acceptable. I will take anything.

Just to avoid more annoying corrections from my former boss, I carefully retie the ice bag and latch the cooler.

I flip the metal lid of the crusher over the ice and examine the hand crank.

This doesn't look too hard. You clearly turn the handle so the grinders will break up the ice, and the beautiful slush falls into the bowl.

I realize it might splash my precious margarita mix onto the table, but it's too late to fix that problem, so I go for it and begin cranking the handle.

It doesn't budge.

Maybe I'm going the wrong way. I push it in the other direction.

Still nothing.

The crank is not at a great height for me, requiring me to lift my arm higher than I can really put leverage behind, so I stand on the cooler.

Rhett half-turns, and I can sense his desire to tell me not to break the cooler.

"Don't," I warn him.

He sensibly stays quiet.

At this point, it's *margaritas or murder.*

From my perch, I can grasp the handle with both hands and push down. It moves a fraction of an inch, and I get the satisfying sound of ice crunching. A couple of tidbits drop into the bowl.

"Success!" I shout.

I put all my energy into a second push and get three more dribbles of crushed ice.

Hmm. That's not much result for my effort. This is hard.

I push again, and a few more particles of ice fall into the bowl.

I step down to peer at my progress, but the few ice bits are almost melted already, given the warmth of the island-temperature mix.

I need to get this cranking.

I step back up and push the handle with all my might. This time it gets a good quarter turn, and more ice falls to the bottom.

"Yes!"

Except now the crank has to go up to keep going around. This is much harder than pushing down on it.

I grunt and I groan, but no matter how much effort I put into the upward swing, I can't get the handle to budge.

This sucks.

I open the top and peer in. There is plenty of ice inside. I use my cup to move it around, wondering if a piece of ice is stuck. But no, it all fluidly moves in and around the gears that draw it down into the grinder.

Now I understand why they had the most buff member of the crew on crank duty. He made it look easy.

But it's hard. Really hard.

No.

It's not.

It's a challenge, and I *thrive* on challenge.

You've got this, Bailey.

I shift myself beneath the handle so that I have more room to thrust upward and get the crank to go.

No luck.

Dang it.

I want to cry. I want a margarita. I *need* a margarita.

I dip my cup into the bowl and skim off the bits of crushed ice that have survived.

I take a drink. Whoa. It's way too strong. It's going to need a mountain of ice.

"How is it?" Rhett asks.

"It's perfect." I take another drink in defiance.

Could things get any worse? A beautiful private island, ruined. A glorious amount of margarita mix all to myself, unusable.

Tears prick the corners of my eyes. Is this going to be the thing that defeats me? An ice crusher?

I don't think so.

Rhett takes a step toward me. "I can crank it—"

I hold up a hand. "Rhett Armstrong, get away from me. I am *Bailey motherfucking Johansson*, and I am going to make myself a margarita if it kills me."

He takes a step back. "Just trying to help."

I examine the handle for a moment. I think if I get on the other side of the machine, I'll have more leverage than trying to push through it. I drag the cooler around the shredded plastic skirt of the table.

Then I stand on it, grasp the handle from this angle, and thrust upward with all my might.

It moves!

I realize I need to keep going. It's the starting that's hard, not the momentum.

I push the crank down, and this time, do not let go for anything.

It rolls all the way around.

And then again.

Ice falls into the bowl.

I crank and crank and crank and crank until there is no more ice coming out and the crank spins freely.

The bowl is half full, the water and ice fusing together in that magical slush we had when the food crew was here. I drag my cup through it to mix it better. I don't care that I've drunk from the cup already. It's *my* bowl of margaritas.

Mine.

I take a sip from my cup. It's delicious. I nailed it.

I sit on the cooler and take a deep, glorious swig. I hold it in my mouth for a second, not wanting a brain freeze to mess up this moment, and let the flavors of lime and tequila wash away my misery.

Only when I've calmed down considerably do I turn to look at Rhett. He's leaning against the inside of the hut, watching me with bemusement. "Is it the best margarita you've ever had?" he asks.

"You bet your sweet ass it is."

"You sharing?"

"I don't know. You might get dehydrated."

He nods. "How about we call a truce?"

"We tried that earlier."

"Well, we decided not to talk about work. I'm still ornery as hell."

I almost spit my drink. "That you are. It's good to be self-aware."

"So, are you sharing?"

I scoot over on my perch on the cooler. "All right. Come sit by me."

20

RHETT

Bailey dunks my cup into her bowl of margaritas and passes it, dripping, to me.

"Cheers," she says, tapping her paper cup against mine.

We drink amongst the mud and broken limbs of the hut, the sun pouring down from the missing roof.

Common sense tells me we should find some shade. Move the bowl of crushed ice to a place where it will melt more slowly. Figure out a timeline for eating and drinking the supplies that we have in case our rescue is delayed.

But I shove it all aside. I've said enough already. Instead, I soak in the early evening light, sip the perfectly slushed drink, and try to imagine that this interlude with this woman at this location is exactly where I always planned to be.

A breeze rushes in from the ocean, circling through the hut. The saltwater scent returns, pushing away the smell of rain as if nothing unexpected has happened today.

Bailey tucks a wild lock of hair behind her ear. She has a smudge of mud on her jaw. I resist the urge to reach out and wipe it off.

I think of her pink lip gloss, the *pop* sound her mouth made after she put it on at her desk.

Nope. Gotta let that go.

I force myself to picture the yacht skimming across the ocean, the crew and my employees unaware that their boss and his former assistant have been left behind.

"What are you thinking?" Bailey asks. "I can't sit in silence for long."

I know this about her. "I'm wondering who's going to be the first to figure out that we got left behind."

"Gloria, for sure," Bailey says.

"That's a good choice. I'd take that bet, except I scared her off from my room."

"Surprise, surprise." Bailey swirls her cup, staring into its depths. "Rhett Armstrong acts like an ogre."

She isn't going to pull any punches at this juncture.

I brace my elbows on my knees. "So give it to me straight. What were my worst qualities as a boss?"

I can see her fighting to avoid smiling. "Well, I guess we *do* have all day, so I could get started on this lengthy list."

"Maybe it's quicker to say if I had any good qualities at all."

She tilts her head, her dark eyes meeting my gaze. "That's a considerably shorter conversation."

"So, anything?"

She shrugs. "People look up to you. You'd be surprised how rare that can be."

I suppose they do. But it always seemed to me that was only because they had to. I held their employment future in my hands.

"You always kept the job interesting," she continues. "Office work can be tedious. The same thing, over and over. But with you, we always had new skills to learn and try."

That's true. "It's because we've been in a constant growth cycle since we started."

"Plenty of people would say your best quality is that you run a good business. It's profitable. That's more than a lot of businesses can say."

This is better than I expected. "And the downsides?"

"But there's so many." She sips her drink again.

"What is the absolute worst one?"

She shakes her head. "Nobody ever really wants to know that."

"I do."

She narrows her eyes at me. "Why is this important?"

"This is a rare opportunity. Someone who worked with me for two years, whom I then fired, who is now stuck with me on a private island. You can't duplicate the scenario."

"I could walk down the beach and avoid you until someone comes for us."

"You could. It wouldn't be wise. We need to stay close to this area because this is where they'll expect us to be."

Bailey lets out a little *grrrr* sound. "I can take the shed, and you can keep the hut."

"You would never abandon your margaritas."

She turns to look at the ice crusher with affection. "I could make off with the bowl, but the ice crusher looks permanent."

"So what is it? My worst trait."

She sighs. "Fine. But don't murder me on an abandoned island."

I press my hand to my heart. "I solemnly swear not to murder you on this island."

"All right. Here it is." She takes another gulp, probably for courage. "You don't acknowledge the things you don't know. Either you don't know you don't know them. Or you're so full of yourself that you think you can get by without knowing them."

I think about her words. Is that true? "But…" I search for how to say this. "Isn't it hard for me to know if you're right, because I don't know what I don't know?"

"Well, now you do."

"Do what?"

"Know that you don't know. I gave you the red pill. You ate the apple of the forbidden tree. Go forth and learn!"

I can't help but grin at her. She seems so frustrated with me, like she used to get in the office. "So, you're doing me a favor here?"

"Absolutely. But it didn't help me when the time came."

That sobers me. I take a long pull of the margarita

before I respond to that. "You mean the marketing snafu." It's not a question.

"In that particular case," she says, her eyes on her cup, "neither of us knew what we were doing."

I lean back against the metal stand holding the ice crusher. "We agreed not to talk about this until we were back on the ship."

"We did."

"You think we should do it now?"

She shrugs. "We don't have any paperwork. I have no corroborating data. I don't know how I can prove anything to you."

"I might have that on the ship. Gloria ran the dailies on paper for me so that I could review everything that went down leading up to Viola bringing me the requisitions."

She turns to me at that. "Why did you do that? You already let me go."

"Maybe I was trying to figure out what I don't know."

"You could've done that before you had me escorted out."

She's right. "I could have."

"So that leads us to the second worst thing about you. Your snap decisions suck. I had to go in behind you and clean up several of them."

I sit up straighter at that. "Like when?"

"Like when you outsourced IT and literally no one's computers worked for three weeks."

"We lost too much staff. I couldn't get people hired and trained in time."

"I know. You made a snap decision. Let's hire an IT company to bridge the gap." Her voice rises in pitch.

"It was a solid decision."

"But you signed a *contract*. And then when they couldn't handle our needs, and when you hired people back in the end, we had to float a huge tech budget that was completely unnecessary."

"What would you have done?" I ask.

"I would have known to ask for help. To get an expert in. Not to just fill the gap with my limited knowledge. You talk about this half a million in marketing I got fired over, that was half a million you wasted. Nobody fired *you* over it. I assume you're untouchable with Dougherty."

She's not wrong.

I'm not sure I want to hear any more. I stand up, draining my cup and setting it on the stand. "I'm going to clear more of this brush so we can walk around."

"Is that a snap decision?" Her voice has a hard edge.

I turn around to face her. "Why? Is it a bad one?"

"Absolutely. We have priorities. We should move the cooler to the shed, where it's protected from the sun. There's no point in clearing this hut because the only advantage it has over the shed is the sink and an ice crusher. We can utilize both of these easily by walking over here and save ourselves the sun and the accelerated melting of the ice by being protected the rest of the time."

Why is she always right?

I nod. "Okay, let's move the cooler to the shed."

Baily holds up a palm. "Not until I finish this margarita."

Good God. This is the most maddening woman on the planet.

And I'm stuck with her.

21

BAILEY

I sure love annoying Rhett Armstrong.

I don't budge until the entire bowl of margaritas is consumed. Rhett is considerably more smiley by the time we're through it.

By then, though, it matters a lot less that we move to the shed. The sun is headed into the sea, the lingering storm clouds in the distance turning the sky the most vivid orange-red sunset I've ever seen.

I dig my phone out of my bag and walk toward the ocean to snap the shot. The image barely does it justice.

Rhett stands next to me. "Storms make the sky more colorful, although maybe it's so beautiful because you survived it."

I smack his arm. "Who knew Rhett Armstrong could be poetic!"

He shrugs. "We're the only two people on the planet who get to see it."

Now that's something to consider. Whatever

happens here can never be documented or known to a single other person unless we tell them.

"Come on," I tell him. "Let's make more margaritas and sit on the dock."

So we do, taking our drinks along with the oysters and a cup of pickle juice.

We sit on the last unbroken section, watching the sun go down. I discover that if I drown the oyster in pickle juice, slurp it quickly, then follow it with a swig of margarita, I can manage them.

"We should eat what we can," Rhett says. "I don't trust them after they sit out all night."

"Could we cook them? Would that make them last longer?"

"I think so, especially if they stay cold after." He tips another shell into his mouth. It's interesting, watching his long throat move. He's showing a shadow of a beard. He's going to look way off his clean-cut self if we're here for long.

I kind of look forward to this.

He sets the shell in the tray. "If we're going to make a fire, we should do it before it gets full dark. I think this night is going to be the blackest black we've ever seen."

"How much power does your phone have to use as a flashlight?" I ask him.

He pulls it out of the pocket of his swim trunks. "Forty percent."

"I'm at fifty-eight. I'll keep it powered all the way off except when we use it for light."

He nods.

And yet, still, we sit there a little longer, watching the sun.

It's quiet and peaceful, and for a moment, I can imagine that this isn't a disaster. That I'm here with my great love, and we chose this for a perfect solitary honeymoon, and the world is completely at bay.

I lean toward him as if I might rest my head on my shoulder.

Whoa, Bailey. You've had one too many.

I jump to my feet. "I guess I'll look for anything dry to burn for the fire. Do you have tips?"

He seems amused at my sudden burst of energy. "I'd go for twigs and small limbs that were out in the sun after the storm. If we get a good blaze going, we can dry out the rest."

I dust sand off my legs and leave the dock to collect brushy debris. Some of it is wet, but when I shake it, the limbs seem dry enough.

Rhett walks by with the bowl and the oysters he didn't finish to take to the shed.

"How are we going to start the fire?" I ask him.

"I can get a spark going with one of the metal tools in the shed. We need kindling."

I'm relieved he has a plan. "I'll get more."

There isn't much to scavenge on the beach, so I head to the tree line, where small branches and uprooted bushes lie around everywhere.

Rhett and I were a good team back in the day, when he wasn't being a raging maniac. I get that old familiar feeling of working with him as I drop my pile of brush outside the shed and head inside. The dark is falling rapidly.

I hope we can get the fire started before it's impossible to see. This is my fault. I insisted on margaritas when we should have been using our daylight wisely. Rhett isn't the only one who makes bad decisions.

Inside the shed, Rhett opens and closes drawers. "The damp brush won't be easy to light with a spark. I wish we had paper."

"My notebook!" I rotate my bag around where it's slung across my back.

"Right. You're full of ideas tonight."

"It's the margaritas," I say.

And it might be true. The edge is off my fear, my annoyance, my impatience. It might be helping Rhett, too. He's smiling an awful lot for a man stranded on a deserted island.

"Should I crumple the paper?" I tear out blank pages.

"Yes," Rhett says. "We want to create a tight but easily sparked ball that we can use to light bigger pieces, gradually working up to branches."

"I'll go find bigger ones."

"If it's fat, bring it even if it's wet. We can strip off the damp exterior."

I nod and head to the tree line one more time, my flip-flops kicking up sand.

Whoa, it's getting dark. I decide to use some of my phone power, examining the tree branches for good candidates.

I find several loose ones that are small enough for me to manage and head back.

When I return, Rhett is blowing into a wad of the paper. It's smoking!

"How did you do it?"

"A hammer and a rock." He tilts his head toward a collection of rocks at his feet. "Took a minute to find the right rock to make a spark."

I drop the limbs next to the pile of brush. "Rhett Armstrong, were you a Boy Scout?"

He blows into the paper wad until it glows red. "Maybe."

When the wad is clearly starting to burn, he nestles it into a clump of tiny branches. We watch it, praying it won't go out. The light is fading fast.

A stick catches, then another.

"Quickly, let's cover it with more loose sticks," he says.

I break off dozens of twigs, spreading them over the branches.

"Did you find thicker ones?" he asks.

I nod and push several closer to him. It's getting hard to see them. "Should we use my phone?"

"We're all right. We'll have good light in a minute." He establishes the boundaries of the fire with the bigger limbs, pulling off the damp outer bark of some of them.

Smoke shows up as gray against the night. The smell of burning wood replaces the tang of the ocean.

The fire makes me feel better.

"Is the metal bowl empty?" Rhett asks.

"You want me to make another round?" He's definitely not being boss Rhett now. My tongue feels loose, and I will my brain not to accidentally call him Mr. Juicy.

"Maybe put some pickle brine in it," he says. "Then we can cook the oysters. It's metal, so it will work well on the fire."

"Oysters in pickle brine. We could start a cookbook for stranded castaways." I head into the shed to dunk a cup in the pickle bucket.

As I walk away, he chuckles. Huh! He's laughing!

When the fire is blazing, we pour pickle brine into the bowl and lay the last oysters inside.

Rhett nestles the bowl on the fire.

"How are we going to take it off when it's hot?" I ask.

He turns to pick up a metal-handled mop. "I'll scoot it off with this."

"You've thought of everything." I spot a beach towel flapping in the shadows and retrieve it from a twisted lounger. It's dry.

I spread it on the ground. "Now we can sit on something that isn't sand."

Rhett grunts. "We probably won't get much sleep."

Even as he says it, though, I feel the pull of exhaustion taking over. The confrontations, the sun, the storm. It's been a lot.

The towel isn't big enough for two unless we're seated, but I curl into a tight ball, my head by Rhett's thigh, my feet in the sand.

The flickering light of the fire and the sizzle of the oysters in the juice lull me to sleep.

22

RHETT

It's something, watching Bailey sleep.

I think of campfires as a kid, eating s'mores and crashing after the sugar rush on sleeping bags encircling the pit.

Our family was outdoorsy. We pitched a lot of tents and spent many nights under the stars. We lived in upstate New York, where it's prime camping during the warm months, as long as you avoid the ticks.

My parents live in Colorado now, on a plot of land next to my younger brother Axel. He made outdoor life his vocation.

Wealth from selling his app didn't change him. And he hikes like he always did. Naked.

Our parents definitely didn't teach him that.

But this night feels different from when I was a kid.

I'm in charge, for one. I was often the slacker on camp-outs. Dad and Axel were enthusiastic, setting up camp just to suit them.

Mom was the organizer, making sure we had food and cookware and sleeping bags and proper outfits.

My brother Court and I mostly goofed off during these expeditions. Our baby sister Nadia was young in the years I was still going, so she wasn't much help either.

But Dad and Axel, they were something to behold. Stringing up clotheslines. Bear-proofing. Fishing. Setting up a massive fire pit complete with a cooking rack.

Dad was a Boy Scout leader, of course. He made all of us boys be Scouts.

My skills are rusty, but they are coming in handy.

I don't know how long oysters need to cook on a fire, but as the water boils away, I figure they must be done. It's important to have food to ration.

I try not to think grim thoughts about the boat taking too long to get to us. I may have built a fire, but long-term survival is not part of my knowledgebase.

I nudge the bowl out of the ashes with the broom handle. My movement sets off something in Bailey because she shifts on the towel, and her head ends up lying on my thigh.

She murmurs happily and snuggles in.

My pulse leaps. This is a pretty intimate situation. Things would've been different if I hadn't fired her. We wouldn't have had the altercation on the beach. She probably would have built her castle near the other employees.

I wouldn't have taken off the wrong way and been so far out.

When everyone got evacuated, we'd have been with them.

And she would have brought Maxwell, I suppose.

Maybe I would've met him. Maybe I would have even liked him. Hung out, like I did with Sarah and Caleb.

No. No way.

What's happening right now, with Bailey sleeping practically in my lap, feels like I'm encroaching on his girl. I need to put some distance between us.

Besides, after all the margaritas during the day, my bladder is screaming.

I slide my hand beneath Bailey's head, amazed at how silken her hair feels after all it's been through today. Rainwater as shampoo. No wonder it's so commonly used in marketing.

I slip out from beneath her and carefully rest her head on the towel. She murmurs again, but she doesn't wake up.

We haven't addressed the bathroom situation since the hut was destroyed. Maybe we won't need to. It's a big enough island with two people. It's not like we need to organize latrine spots.

The moonlight is strong enough for me to pick my way across the littered beach, but when I get to the tree line, it's pitch black. I have to use some of my precious battery power.

Once I figure out where I'm aiming, I flip the light off.

The quiet is almost complete in the trees. I consider what wildlife might be on this island. Birds, probably. I haven't seen any, not even seagulls. But maybe the local birds stay more deeply in the interior.

Iguanas could be prevalent here. And I assume there will be some sort of insects. The fire should keep those away, I hope.

The sound of my pee hitting leaves seems incredibly loud in the silence. If a man pees on an island and nobody hears him, did he really—

A snap of twigs startles me. I lift my head, peering into the blackness.

Then, a few seconds later, another one.

It's big, whatever it is. But there can't be any large predators on this island. It's too small. But a wild boar? Wild pig?

No, they wouldn't be easing through the trees. They are prey. They'd crash through the underbrush like Pumba in *The Lion King*.

I'm not sure if I should call out or be quiet. I think the pee is done, but then a muscle twitches, sending another spray going.

Great. The sound is like a signpost in the quiet, and I can't shut it off.

There's another quick snap. I don't know if I should turn on my light. I could scare off whatever it is.

My pulse quickens. Whatever lives on the island isn't used to having humans here at night. That's for sure. Nothing about this place is set up for it.

Mercilessly, the flow of urine finally stops. I'm about to tuck things away when I'm blinded by a bright light.

"What the hell?" I call.

Bailey shrieks. She gasps. She fumbles with her

phone. Light skitters through the trees, illuminating fallen branches and brush. "Sorry! So sorry!" The phone drops to the ground, and she squints her eye as she picks it up, the bright glare in her face.

Then it's off. I can't see anything other than splotches of gray where my eyes were seared by the unexpected brightness.

Then I say, "Are you okay?"

I don't think I'll address whatever body parts she might've seen.

"You…left me. Alone. On an island. At night." Her voice wavers.

"I'm sorry. The bathroom hut is—"

"No. I get it. I get it. I'm sorry. I don't know why I didn't think of that. I'm just…" She still breathes hard. "Overwhelmed, I think. This is a lot."

"What can I do?"

"Give me a second."

I wait her out. I can't see her at all.

Finally, I say, "I'm gonna flip on my light for a second so we can get back to the beach. There's moonlight there, but here we can trip over things."

"Okay."

I lead us out of the brush. We pause at the edge of the sand, letting our eyes adjust to the dim moonlight.

I decide a change of subject might be best. "Tomorrow we might want to prioritize making a path through the debris. We don't want to get injured."

"Okay." Her voice is still breathless as she glances back at the trees.

Before I can think of how embarrassing this question might be for her, I ask, "Do you need to go?"

She shakes her head furiously. "I'm waiting for daylight. We don't know what's out there."

"I don't think there's anything out there, but if you can wait, that's not a bad idea."

We walk along the beach, picking our way around lounge chairs and palm leaves.

"You could always go in the ocean, I guess," I say. This is the weirdest conversation I've ever had with a woman.

"I guess so. It seems weird, but it's a lot of water." Then she stops. "It wouldn't attract sharks, would it?"

"Urine? No. Even the blood part is a myth."

Now I've made it even worse by mentioning more bodily fluids.

"I'm not—"

"Okay." I don't want to talk about this.

We make it back to the shed. The fire is as we left it. I pick up the bowl and shine a light into it to make sure no aforementioned insects have discovered our food. It's clear.

"I should put these away."

"Sorry I fell asleep on you."

"We have to sleep."

She darts a few feet away, and my instinct is to grab her arm to keep her safe.

She returns with another towel. "We should collect more of these tomorrow. They'll be helpful in case we get wet or get sick of sitting in sand."

"And we should redouble our efforts to find working loungers."

Her laugh is half grunt. "You get to test them."

"Fair enough."

She repacks the cooled oysters into one of the trays.

"Should we try one?" Bailey asks. "Make sure there's some validity to our future best-selling castaway cookbook?"

I consider where my hands have just been and how far it is to a sink. "I think I'm going to wait until tomorrow," I say. "You're welcome to."

"Actually, you're right. I'm more tired than hungry."

We head inside the shed to the cooler.

Bailey makes a pile out of life jackets and spreads the second towel over it. "I feel safer in here," she says. "Four walls and a roof."

"That's fine. I'll watch the fire."

"Okay." She lays her head down, but her eyes don't close.

It's going to be a fitful night, that's for sure. I sit at the threshold of the open double doors. I want to make sure the fire is fed enough to at least stay in embers until morning. It would be nice not to have to start over when it comes time to boil water to drink.

And as the hours pass, I find most of them are spent thinking about the woman lying on a lumpy makeshift bed a few feet away.

23

BAILEY

I can't sleep.

I watch Rhett's silhouette in front of the fire. He's outside the shed.

My pile of life jackets is way worse to sleep on than the towel.

Earlier I dreamed I was cuddled up to Rhett, safe and secure, then I woke up and realized he was gone.

My panic in that moment was second only to the moment in the storm when I curled in a ball in the hut. I thought I was alone then, too.

But in the woods, I saw him. Saw parts of him no assistant should see of her boss.

The swim trunks slung low, his flat belly ending in…

Yeah, don't think about that.

But I am now. It seems like our fighting is spent. Rhett admits he acted too hastily. He was investigating the marketing issue before the cruise.

He's not a bad person. But like I told him, he assumes he knows everything, that he's infallible.

He's learning he's not.

I close my eyes and count to one hundred, hoping I can lose myself in sleep.

But I keep drifting to thoughts of Rhett. His laugh. The way he listened this time, brows drawn in concentration. And so much of him, bare and out there for me to see.

I'm back to that.

I give up on sleeping and roll away from the pile of jackets.

Rhett turns. "Can't sleep?"

"Nope."

I spread the second towel next to the first. "They'll come tomorrow, right?"

"I would think so, unless nobody notices we're gone until the cruise is over."

"So that would be one more night, then however long it takes for them to get here."

"Right. So the day after tomorrow, for sure."

"If they have a boat close."

"That, too."

"Do you think we should prepare as if they're never coming?" I dislike the tremble in my voice, but the question is a hard one.

"We could, I guess. Do you mean figure out a way to fish or catch small game or eat coconuts?"

"Sure. We already have shelter."

"I wouldn't worry too much. They're going to know where we are. They know how to get here. It's not like we got lost at sea or had a plane crash no one can track."

His eyes watch me with a combination of compassion and concern that hit me deep down. Whatever we were before as a boss who drove me crazy and an assistant who disappointed him, we're not that anymore. We're two humans, cut off from the world, figuring out how to get by.

When I first worked for him, he was much more laid-back, more like he is now. I actually had quite a thing for him. This was how Viola and I became friends. We had a mutual obsession.

But within two weeks of working for him, everything changed.

Rhett got stiff and formal and found fault with everything I did. Frankly, his demands were ridiculous. Get this report in by noon, when it was impossible. Get the answer for this thing that would have been a challenge for someone with more experience and training.

I did my best to rise to the occasion. I endured. I worked. I never considered quitting. Rhett's harshness was mitigated by the fact that I had made friends at Dougherty. Viola and I were inseparable. And I got to know everyone quickly. I kept track of their lives and their personal details, partly to help Rhett. But also because I liked doing it. I liked knowing who I worked with.

When he fired me, he didn't only prove that he didn't value all the things that I had done. He cut me off from the work and the people I enjoyed.

And here we are. But the Rhett I'm seeing now, drinking margaritas, making a fire—that's the Rhett I remember from the beginning. And I'm pretty sure that's the Rhett he's meant to be. That everything else is some kind of weird act.

But I have to ask the hardest question of all. "What if nobody reports us as missing? What if nobody cares?"

His head turns ever so slowly to pierce me with his gaze. "You have family. So do I." He hesitates a beat, then says, "And of course you have Maxwell."

This gets my attention. "Maxwell? I mean, he's the love of my life, but I don't think he will even notice I'm gone as long as he's fed and has a warm place to sleep."

"Really?" Rhett seems flabbergasted.

Geez, you'd think he never heard of a cat before. Maxwell, well, he is what you would affectionately call *aloof*. And if you cross him, he can be a terror.

But to Rhett, I say, "He's been like that since the beginning. Over time, I thought he'd get more affectionate, but it never happened. He won't even get on my bed."

Now Rhett sits bolt upright. "He doesn't sleep with you?"

I'm not so sure why Rhett is stuck on this point. "I mean, every once in a while, I'll be sitting on the couch, and he'll get on the other end of it. But that tends to be about as close as he gets to me."

Rhett stares at me in something that looks like shock. "And this is okay with you?"

I shrug. "I don't think there's much I can do to change it. It's just the way he is."

Rhett tears his gaze from me and stares into the fire. "I can't imagine living that way." He seems deep in thought. Agitated, too, judging by the way his thumb rapidly taps his thigh.

I don't get it. "Rhett? Why are you so surprised at this? Did you think I would have perfect pets or something? A lot of cats are like Maxwell."

His head snaps to me. "Maxwell is your cat?"

"Yeah. I've had him for six years."

His entire demeanor changes. He rocks backward, laughing into the sky. "Maxwell is a cat!"

"Did you think he was a dog? I had a picture of him on my desk."

"I remember the cat picture. But I didn't know that was Maxwell."

"Who did you think Maxwell was?"

Rhett won't look at me.

"Wait, did you think Maxwell was my boyfriend?" My laugh is loud against the snapping of the fire. "You did! You thought my cat was a boyfriend who wouldn't sleep with me."

We both lose it. Rhett falls back in the sand. I double over, my giggles erupting into a full-on belly laugh.

We're like this for several long minutes until my laughter dissolves into hiccups. I hold my breath to get rid of the hiccups, then we start to sober up.

I wipe tears from my eyes. "Did you think Maxwell was my boyfriend the whole time I worked for you?"

He straightens a corner of the towel. "Pretty much. You first mentioned him the second week you worked for me."

Everything in my belly goes still. That's about when he started acting weird. Surely there wasn't a connection. Why would him thinking that I had a boyfriend make him act so standoffish and harsh?

But then, Viola's face rises in my vision, saying, "I think he has a thing for you."

I'm not laughing now. "Rhett, did you ever have a conversation with Viola about me and Maxwell?"

He leans over to grab a log, stripping the wet bark from the outside before throwing it onto the fire.

"I don't talk to Viola much. I got the impression I should keep my distance."

That is a wise assessment. At least he's aware of her potential treachery.

"So, you two never discussed it?" I really need to know.

"We did, once, in passing. We were in the elevator together. She mentioned you were going with her to some beach concert that weekend and asked if I wanted to come along."

I remember that concert. It was one of the last things I did with Viola before I got fired. "I'm assuming you turned her down."

"I asked if she was looking for a date since you would be with Maxwell."

Interesting. "What did she say to that?" Viola knows Maxwell is my cat.

"Just that Maxwell wouldn't be there."

"And then?"

"I'm not sure I remember. It wasn't a particularly memorable conversation. She might've been uncharacteristically quiet, like she had a lot going on inside her head."

It's possible I should have some allegiance to Viola. We were best friends for two years. But I don't feel it. Not anymore.

"I knew Viola pretty well," I say.

"Of course. You guys were always together."

"Yeah, up until she got me fired."

Rhett's fingers fiddle with a piece of brush. "She was upset when she turned those papers in. She begged me not to fire you."

"That doesn't mean she meant it. I'm trying to trace the timeline of everything."

"What do you mean?"

"If she was talking about that beach concert we went to, that was only two weeks before she came to you with the so-called evidence that I cost the company half a million in fraudulent marketing charges."

"That sounds about right."

"She's had this massive obsession with you for years."

He scrunches his brow. "I recently realized that."

"Right. Because she snuck up to your cabin."

Rhett puffs out an angry rush of air. "Does everyone know about that?"

"I don't think so. I saw her leaving your floor after I talked to Kenna about it. Kenna is her new bestie, although her allegiance isn't particularly strong."

"So you and Viola aren't friends anymore?"

"Hell no. Not that I initiated that. Viola cut me off. She knows what she did."

Rhett breaks twigs off a piece of brush with angry snaps. "So, you think my conversation with Viola about

Maxwell and the beach concert led to her getting you fired?"

"I mean, I don't get the connection. Why would you care if I had a boyfriend or a cat? But it meant some-thing to her. There's no reason why she did it on this timeline, except for that conversation. If she was going to get me jettisoned, she could have done it at any time."

Rhett releases a shower of crumbled twig bits to the sand. "And nothing else happened between you two? There was no reason why she might want to get you out of the company?"

"I mean, who knows with Viola? We did everything together. It was like a break-up for me. And then with no job? My life got completely upended."

He brushes his hands together to knock the twig dust off. "I can see that. I'm sorry. I'm not sure where we go from here, though."

"First, we have to get off this island."

He nods.

But something tickles in the back of my brain. Viola realized that Rhett thought I had a boyfriend. She didn't know that before, or she would have brought it up. She would've found it hysterical. The perfect office gossip.

But if she believed he was interested in me, and that maybe the only thing holding him back was the fact that I had a boyfriend, that misconception was important.

If he figured it out, maybe he would ask about it, and I could tell him. And then he would be…what? Free to ask me out?

Oh, God. Really?

No.

Not possible. I suck in a breath and press my hand to my throat.

Rhett turns to me. "What?"

"I think I know what Viola was thinking."

"And?"

"She wanted you. And she realized, or at least she thought, that the only thing holding you back from dating me was the fact that I had a boyfriend. Which I didn't. She didn't want you to find out. That would have hurt her chances for whatever scheme she had to get you. So she got me kicked out of the company."

Only after I've said all this do I realize that I have suggested that this man, my former boss, who made me nothing but miserable for the better part of two years, is actually into me. Into me enough to be a threat to someone who wanted him for herself.

I backtrack. "That's crazy." I wave into the night. "Court reporter, please strike that from the record. That was false testimony. Forget it."

I can't seem to stop myself. I hold an imaginary object in front of Rhett's face. "I'm the Men in Black. Please stare into this light, so that you don't remember what just happened." I make a buzzing sound.

I'm making this worse, but I'm so embarrassed. I've made a huge assumption. A terrible one. One that can't be true.

Rhett hasn't said anything. He stares into the fire.

"I'm so sorry. That was presumptuous of me. Obviously, Viola had some other motivation to kick me out of the company. That was outrageous and borderline narcissistic. And I wish I hadn't said it. Please tell me you've already forgotten it."

He's still quiet.

The silence is killing me, and I can't stop my mouth from running. "I would walk away and go somewhere else, but there's nowhere to go."

Another long minute passes. God. He must think I'm insane.

I want to rewind the last five minutes, completely shut my damn mouth. Even if I thought these things, I should have kept them to myself. This wild theory involving him liking me romantically should have stayed in my head.

Rhett clears his throat.

I completely don't expect his next words.

"Viola was right."

24

RHETT

I t's a real wonder, watching Bailey's expression change with my admission.

At first, her eyes grow wide. Then she casts her gaze down to the sand.

I don't know what she's thinking. I may have made our time on the island super awkward.

I should fix it. "I'm sorry. That didn't need to be said aloud."

She fiddles with the edge of the beach towel. "So, Viola was right about how you feel about me?"

"I thought I was masking it. But obviously not well enough."

"Why would you mask it?"

"Because you seemed to be madly in love with this Maxwell."

She bursts out laughing, and relief washes over me that we're okay.

"I *am* madly in love with Maxwell." Now she looks me in the eye. "Are you telling me I endured two years of your absolute ogre-ness because you *like* me? Like we're in third grade? Were you planning on pulling my braids?"

"You never wear braids, Bailey."

"Rhett Armstrong!" Her tone is stern. "You owe me more of an explanation than that."

She's right. "I had to be the boss. And I was already in over my head. I got put in a role I wasn't quite ready for. To get things done, I put on a lot of personalities trying to find the right fit."

"The only personality anyone needs is *their* personality."

"You say that, but I wasn't exactly known for my business decorum. Or my work ethic. Or even being on time."

"No way. You were the warden, making everyone behave."

"Mainly because I was making my inner slacker behave."

She shakes her head. "I find this hard to believe. You set a standard that was impossible to live up to."

I know she's right. "This is what happens when you're not cut out for a role you've been given."

The ends of her hair are lit up from the fire. The shifting light dances across her skin. "Then why did you take the job if it's so ill-suited to you?"

Yeah, this is dangerous. I want to tell her everything.

Do everything.

Now that I know there is nothing to hold us back, this conversation is difficult to focus on.

But I've learned discipline in the last two years. I hold onto the last shred of it.

"Let's just say Dougherty was an opportunity I couldn't refuse." No lie there.

Bailey may not be a part of the company anymore, but I still can't reveal a secret as big as Uncle Sherman.

She holds out her arms, stretching. "That I can identify with. I know all about having to stay in a job where your boss makes you miserable because you don't feel you have options."

"I made you feel that way?"

"You were a brute. The worst. But I didn't have a lot of opportunity when I graduated. I'd given up the dream."

This is new. "What dream?"

She draws lines in the sand. "I was naïve about my major. I wasn't cut out for politics. I figured it out."

"I'm sorry that I made you miserable. It was never my intention."

"I'm glad to see you know how to apologize." She grins at me. "You are a human, after all."

"Where do we go from here?"

"Exoneration, maybe?"

She's right. "I should reopen this investigation into why marketing got nothing for a half-million expenditure."

"It sounds like you already have." She stares into the fire. "What are you going to do if you discover it was actually Viola behind all that fraud?"

A limb rolls out of the fire and I poke it back with my broom handle. "You think that's how it will go?"

"I can only assume so. It's beyond what I thought Viola capable of. I mean, she's been treacherous, like you said, with other men at work. But to get me out of the way? When you weren't even interested? I don't know. That's a lot, even for her."

"I have the dailies. I'll get the proof one way or another." I force myself to turn my gaze to her even though I'm feeling pretty chagrined at how the last two years have gone, and my role in it. "I guess we have to decide if you want to be my employee again."

"Why would I want to do that *now*?"

"Because you don't have a job? You just said—"

"Rhett Armstrong, for such a smart man who runs a successful business, the tech debacle notwithstanding, you sure are thick in the head." Her eyes blaze with the firelight. "Do I have to spell it out for you?"

"Maybe?"

"Rhett. There is no Maxwell. The only man I've been fixated on for the last two years was you."

Her words wash over me. Two years of working next to this woman, lost. No touching. No suggestive chatter. No outlet for my feelings.

Yeah, I'm done with that.

I lift her by the waist and set her directly on my lap.

She lets out a little, "Oh!"

Then, when I grab the back of her neck and drag her lips to mine, there's a longer "Ooooh." She melts into me.

Those lips I watched her gloss for years are finally mine. She tastes slightly salty, like the air here, like margaritas. I take all the time I want, learning her mouth from corner to corner.

The world is filled with interruptions, but we will have none here.

But also, I realize, no condoms. No comfortable bed.

I'll make do.

My tongue slips between her lips, and she opens for me. Now it's my turn to dissolve into her. I draw her in, sliding one of her legs around so that she straddles me. My fingers sink into that silky hair I touched so briefly earlier.

I'm drowning in her mouth, her tongue, the heat of her. We're not wearing all that much, and I know the moment she feels me hard against her because she sucks in a breath, her body shivering lightly.

This is my favorite part, accelerating toward the goal.

Her body pressed to mine is a revelation. I have her alone. No office. No barriers. No damn nonexistent boyfriend.

My hands ache to learn every curve of her body. I reach down and circle her ankles with my fingers, squeezing to memorize the distance around them. I rub my thumb against the tender arch of her foot. She groans, and I work them harder, feeling all the tension ease from her.

She hangs onto me, her mouth seeking mine, arms around my neck.

I squeeze her feet and make my way up. I slide my hand along her calves, measuring the swell of her muscle and knocking stray grains of sand from her skin.

The kiss yawns wide, and we fall more fully into each other.

The urge to rush shudders through me, but I set it aside. Tonight is for exploration. Discovery. For chasing down paths that have been built in my mind for years. Destinations I never thought I would actually get to explore.

My fingers make it to her knees, bumping along the hollows like I am reading her body in Braille. There is nothing about her I don't want to know. I slide my fingers along the taut tendon at the base of her hamstring. Nothing is too insignificant to map as the terrain of her.

My pulse quickens as I make my way up her thighs. Her mouth goes still on mine, her breath hitching when my thumbs rest on the edge of her bikini bottom.

She pulls back for a moment, her gaze on mine. I've never seen her eyes like this, glossy and half-lidded, expressing her need.

My throat tightens. "You okay?" I lessen my grip on her thighs.

"I was thinking ahead."

"And?"

She laughs, a ringing sound in the quiet. "I'm on the pill, but I wasn't sure where you were with the condom situation." She glances around. "I have a feeling we're short on those at the moment."

I press a finger just slightly inside the edge of her bikini. "I can do so many things to you that don't involve condoms."

"But if we want to do that…"

"I'll follow your lead."

"When was the last time…"

"Not in months."

"And things seem okay?" She watches my expression.

"All okay."

"So we can do whatever we want, then." She grins.

My dick jumps, and her eyebrows lift. She's right on top of me, with little between us. She felt that.

"We can," I say.

"I might want to do all the things."

"Whatever the lady desires."

"I have to tell you one thing, though."

Her tone makes me pause. Is there something wrong? "Okay."

"I've never had an orgasm. So, don't feel like you did something wrong if it doesn't happen."

"Bailey—"

"I'm serious. Don't feel like you've failed—"

I reach out and shush her with a single finger to her lips. "Bailey, that is about to change. Many, many times."

When I drag her against me, I turn so that she's down on the beach towel. The sand shifts beneath us, conforming to the shape of her body and my elbows and knees, carving out a Bailey-and-Rhett-sized space on this island.

The bikini has a clasp behind her neck, and I flick it open easily. The stretch of the top releases at the lack of tension, and with a quick flip of a second clasp behind her back, it falls away.

I'm ready to worship her. Bailey dresses conservatively at work, all silk blouses and pantsuits. I've seen precious little, rarely even cleavage, and the feast is right here.

She arches her back as I hold her breasts in both hands. The firelight flickers over her body, leaving bright peaks and shadows that I memorize.

When my mouth closes over a pale nipple, Bailey sucks in a breath, her hands curled near her ears. Her hair is spread over the bright colors of the towel, muted in the dark. "This is a sight," I say, feathering kisses from one breast to the other.

"Is it?" She lets out a gasp as I take in the other side.

"I've been longing for this view for a long time."

Her voice is ragged as I make my way down her belly. "The whole time?"

"Mmmm." I slide a finger along the top edge of her bikini bottom. "Since Gloria brought you into my office for your first interview."

"Really?"

The bottom is held with similar clasps to the top, one on each hip. "Mmm hmm." I flick one open. "You were wearing a dark burgundy dress with a black jacket."

"They didn't quite match. I got them at a thrift store."

"When you sat down and crossed your legs, the skirt caught on your knee and revealed some of your thigh before you straightened it."

"You remember that?"

I open the second clasp. "I remember everything."

"What did you think of me then?"

"I was worried about working closely with someone that set me off like you did."

"I did?" She sounds like she doesn't quite believe it, like no one has told her what an effect she can have.

"I spent half the interview trying to focus on the questions. You were smart and capable, and I could see I would be an idiot not to hire you."

"But." Her voice wavers as I slowly inch the bikini bottom away from her skin.

"I kept wanting to do things like this." I spread her thighs apart and take my first long, slow lick of her. Her body is warm and perfectly wet. I use my thumb to spread her wider. I want farther in.

Her entire body shudders as I take a deeper dive. She's deliciously responsive, her hips lifting to meet me.

And I have all the time in the world.

"Rhett," she murmurs. "Remember, it's okay…"

I lick my finger to ensure there isn't any wayward sand before sliding it inside her. I work her from the inside while flicking my tongue against all the spots I'm learning make her writhe beneath me.

She grabs handfuls of sand, and some of it dusts my shoulders as she realizes what she's done and lets it go. Ah, we are going to be a mess. A naked swim will be perfect after this. I want to watch her orgasm in the moonlight, emerging from the sea like Aphrodite.

"Rhett!" Her voice rises, more urgent as I speed up, curling my finger to add pressure.

Her thighs quiver, her belly tight. I could do this all night, my face buried in her, my gaze lifting to skim her naked body, breasts tipped in firelight, her hair in disarray.

She's a goddess. She's mine. I will make sure we never have to wish for each other across an office desk, unaware of how the other feels.

Her nub swells, and I suck on it. This takes her over the edge. She shouts into the night, my name, her creator, unintelligible sounds. The waves crash behind her voice, the moon rising over the water.

Fuck, this is hot. I've been half in love with her for years, but this is the final straw.

"Rhett, Rhett, Rhett, Rhett." Her body quivers, and her sandy hands grip my hair. "What have you done?"

I think she knows. There's no need to say I told you so.

She relaxes, her body resting back on the towel. "I believe you."

I chuckle. "Good."

She rests an arm on her forehead, then sputters. "Oooh, I'm sandy!"

I laugh, kissing my way back to those perfect breasts. "No sheets to grab. Shall we take a dip to wash off?" I am so going to fuck her in the waves.

"Yes."

I stand and help her up. She looks at my swim trunks. "Without those, though."

"Your wish is my desire."

I pull on the tie, but she pushes my hands away. "Let me."

When she kneels in front of me, her naked body licked by firelight, I'm not sure my dick can get any harder. Every beat of my blood rushes to the same place.

But she's not done. When my trunks hit the sand, her mouth is on me, taking me in. Now it's my hands in her hair, my face to the starry sky.

I will never want to leave here.

She works me to the brink, but I want more of her. All of her. I step back and sweep her into my arms. "I'm going to do unspeakable things to you in the ocean."

She squeals as I dodge the fallen beach chairs and branches. "Rhett Armstrong, you are so wild!"

I slow down in the surf, unable to know for sure if debris lies below the dark water. When we're out waist-deep, I turn her in my arms to face me, her legs around my waist.

The moonlight washes her body in blue. We're wet now, dripping, and I've never wanted anything in my life more than I want her.

She holds onto my neck. "This is the wildest thing I've ever done."

"Let this be the first of many." I shift her against me. "Ready?"

"Hell, yeah, I am."

I hold nothing back when I slam into her.

She lets out a shriek that's lost in the pounding of the surf.

I hold onto her thighs, reveling in the slickness of her body tight around me. The water shifts and moves as I lift her away, then slide her down, away, and back.

Her breasts are even with my mouth, so I capture one. Her body clamps down on me.

"Fuck, Rhett. Jesus!"

I hold her tight against me, gyrating deep inside her. The friction between us sets her off. "Goddamnit, Rhett. Not again. Not again. I can't."

I shift her against me, realizing what's getting her. I double down, grinding our bodies together. She whimpers, clutching my shoulders. "It's happening. Rhett. Oh my God."

And I can feel her body responding, the tightening, the gentle pulse.

When her words crumble into random syllables again, I relinquish my control. I feel her, all the way to the core of me, her thighs, her wet skin, her breasts.

I unleash, the warmth coursing from me to her. The friction becomes silken, and our bodies, for a moment, seem to quiver in time with each other.

I bring her tightly against me, her wet hair sending rivulets down my back. Her face is buried in my neck.

The waves keep coming, sparkling with moonlight, endlessly moving toward the beach in their forever path.

I hold onto Bailey, wondering how and why we waited so long to figure out all our missteps, but knowing, with all the certainty of this ocean endlessly reaching for the shore, that I will never let her go.

25

BAILEY

That was…a lot.

My boss turned nemesis has become something significantly more.

We dodge debris in the moonlight, Rhett carefully steering me away from any dangers.

We spot another towel. Rhett shakes it free of sand.

"Now we have a cover," I say.

"We do." He draws his arm around me.

Back at the fire, we shake the two original towels and spread them out. Neither of us wants to dress in our damp bathing suits, so we lay them over a log and settle onto the towels.

When we lie on our makeshift bed, naked, curled together, and covered this time, sleep comes easily.

Sometime near dawn, I wake to the feel of his hard body spooned around my back, his arm draped over my waist.

The embers glow red, and beyond them, a mist

obscures the ocean. We've made it through a night on the island, and rescue might not come for another one.

Right now, I'm glad.

I try not to move, to let him sleep longer, but he must sense that I'm awake. He leans in close to press a kiss on my hair.

"I think we should have a no-clothes day," he murmurs in my ear.

"That sounds reckless."

His hand strays up my ribs. "Let's be utterly reckless."

It's hard to imagine that this is the same Rhett who berated me for the organization of folders on the backup drive.

But we're different here. All the unimportant things are stripped away.

Including our clothes.

When his hand cups my breast, my entire body lights up. I want to keep doing everything with him, over and over. I feel desperate for it, like a thirst I never quite quenched until last night.

I press my back into him, feeling him hard against my thigh. "Like this," I tell him. "Just like this."

He slides his leg between my knees to give himself some space. His wayward hand slides down to edge a finger inside me.

I suck in a breath. I feel wickedly alive. The sun is rising over the trees, and everything around us is softly lit. There is no cover of darkness, no flickering light. We can see everything.

I watch him work me with practiced strokes. My

breath catches. Why has no one else been this good? Is it the solitude? The sun? The wait?

My hips move against him, wanting him inside me. "Please," I whisper.

He shifts, adjusting the angle of his body, then he's there, buried deep. His fingers keep working me, and I'm flooded with pleasure.

I don't want to close my eyes, watching the day grow bright, the breeze picking up from the ocean and making the palm trees sway.

The mist begins to burn off, revealing the waves and the endless blue of the sea. Rhett moves faster and I clutch the sand, almost laughing that I've made the same mistake all over again.

I feel high, like I've taken some wondrous drug. I'm drunk on sunlight and the salty air. And Rhett, doing that thing again with his fingers until I'm wound up like the string on a yo-yo, waiting for him to let me fly.

He's in control of me. My body and its response are completely in his hands.

He uses his knee to spread my legs wider. More fingers go in, and that's it. I unspool, the breeze brushing against the tips of my nipples, the sand shifting beneath my hip.

Rhett works me from behind and inside and I shout to the sky all the words that break free.

He groans behind me, and we're warm and wet together. I've barely descended to the earth and already, I'm desperate to do it again.

I've never felt so insatiable, so overcome. When he's still, I roll over and push him onto his back. I swing a leg over him, my hair falling down my back as I straddle his body.

"Why do I want to do nothing but this over and over again?" I ask.

He brushes my hair back from my eyes. "Because we waited too long."

I know he needs a minute. I remember how guys work. But I need him again.

I glide my body over him, slippery and full of need.

"Fuck, Bailey," he says as he gets hard again. "The things you do to me."

He reaches for my waist, but I pin his hands down. "I'm going to do whatever I want to you."

He allows it, and I stay astride, moving until he's inside me again.

This time I take it at my own pace, up, down, side to side. I bear down, taking in every inch until our bodies grind together.

I can't seem to get close enough. I look at every part of him now that it's light. The bulges of his shoulders and biceps lead to the strong hands pinned near his ears.

The light plays across his jaw, his neck, and his honed chest. His nipples are small and brown, perfectly centered on each muscle. His belly falls flat and smooth to where I work him, his abs shifting as I move.

I work him hard, sweat popping along my hairline. The urgency becomes a desperate plead from my body. I reach for the relief of it, my eyes squeezed closed in concentration.

My mind conjures flowers blooming, petals opening as I work to the brink of collapse. I never want this to end, but I want it more and more. I gasp, on the verge of breaking down. Why am I so lost? Why do I need this so much?

At last, the strain of it moves into a high, teeming buzz that I feel everywhere simultaneously. My body tightens and I can't even breathe. It's so intense, so hard, so overwhelming. It's like time has stopped.

I hold still, teetering on this brink, high on exhaustion. I open my eyes, seared by the brightness of the morning. Rhett waits, his gaze on me, the skin of his neck and chest red, like when he was so upset yesterday.

It's all the same. That passion. That emotion. Such a fine line between hate and lust.

I take in a gulp of air, a sweet deep breath, and like a cartoon character who has been hovering in the sky after running off a cliff, I start to fall.

Every muscle gives way at once. I scream, the cry so long and so loud that it drowns out the ocean. My skin prickles with pleasure, the breeze, and Rhett's eyes on me.

I don't know where he stands, if he came again or not. I can't think about it. I fall onto him in slow motion, my skin melting into his. My head tucks into that comforting space between his neck and shoulder.

Darkness claws at me. It's too much. My life. The storm. This man. What I want. What I just got.

He draws his arms around me and somehow, despite the new day, the rising heat, and the sand everywhere, I fall asleep again.

26

RHETT

I had no idea Bailey could be like this. If I thought our time by the fire was intense, it was nothing compared to this morning.

My arms hold her in place on my chest, her head on my shoulder. She's sound asleep. I let her stay there, my eye on the fire. As long as the embers are alive, I can stir it back to life.

The sky is bright overhead, and a breeze keeps us cool. I think through our objectives for the day. Food. Water. Stay out of the sun. Wait.

We could clear more of the debris, but after Bailey's cut on the chair, I don't want to risk injury by moving broken things around.

The gauze and tape from yesterday came off during our swim. I'll reapply it today.

No, we can't let anything like that cut happen again before we're rescued. Safety is the number one objective.

I stare up at the palm trees overhead. I'm used to the

idea of coconuts, and I've seen brown ones in stores. They are infamously difficult to open.

But the ones above aren't brown at all. They have a smooth, green exterior. Does this mean they aren't ripe?

Nothing I learned in Boy Scouts taught me about island survival, that's for sure.

I'm not sure we could even get to them. Do they fall, or do they have to be harvested? I curse my reliance on search engines. There is no way to find out anything.

The instinct to figure things out, to plan for the worst-case scenario, is urgent.

I have Bailey to think about, too.

At least we have shelter. A fire. Collected rainwater. Our only real concern soon will be food.

I'm grateful for the pickles. They're salt and electrolytes and a way to stave off hunger pains all in one. We don't have to keep them cold.

We'll need to gather more firewood. Assess the quantity and quality of the water. Come up with a better sleeping arrangement. Maybe we can unstuff the life jackets. We're going to grow weary of feeling gritty.

I can repair a couple of loungers. Get us off the sand.

This is such a far cry from my previous goals for the cruise. The dailies. Avoiding employees. Maintaining my position of authority.

Now, it's just me. Bailey. Basic human needs.

Her leg slides off mine, falling onto the sandy towel. She startles, then lifts her head.

I wait for her to look around and orient herself.

She rubs an eye. "Whoa. I had a wicked dream I

survived a storm on a deserted island, then had wild sex with my boss."

"Do you always wake up witty?"

"Maxwell thinks so."

"Lucky Maxwell." I have to shake my head at myself and the cat mistake. So much lost time.

She shifts to my side and slowly sits up. "I see two problems with your naked day idea. Three, actually."

"And what's that?"

"I'm up to four. One: sunburn. Two: sand. Three: our imminent rescue." She peers into the sky. "You think they can satellite feed us to see if we're here?"

"If so, we've given them quite the show."

"Yikes." She glances around and picks up her bathing suit.

"And what is four?"

"We won't stop having sex. Like at all." She glances pointedly at my groin, which is stirring as I watch her work the clasp of the bikini bottom.

"I don't see number four as a problem."

She grins. "Okay, maybe not. But surely we have things to do. Firewood. Water."

Funny how alike we are. "I guess we should draw up an itinerary."

"I'll type it right up. Hopefully, printer two isn't being cranky today."

Now we're both smiling like it's our best day ever, and maybe it is.

I stand up, willing my dick to get itself under control, and step into my swim trunks.

"Oyster and pickle breakfast?" I ask.

"Oh, joy." Bailey heads into the shed and retrieves her cover-up. "I'll go find the sunscreen while you get the fire going again."

Now that we have this easy truce, it's nice seeing how we work together.

"Sure, boss," I say, and Bailey tosses me a smile that makes me feel as though the sand is shifting beneath my feet.

I find myself whistling as I scour the edge of the tree line for brush and limbs. For the barest second, I imagine never getting rescued. Making clothes out of towels and fabric scavenged from the life jackets.

Scaling the trees for coconuts, or figuring out how to knock them down. Getting a pet parrot and teaching it to cuss. Fishing off the rocks where we had our first and last island fight.

Having little Rhett-Bailey babies.

I catch myself. I'm off the deep end.

We have jobs. Families. And this is only paradise until one of us gets sick or hurt.

By the time I've returned to the fire with a load, Bailey is there, too, spreading sunscreen on her face and arms. "I think I'll skip my legs. Save it for the things that burn the worst. Do you have a shirt somewhere?"

"Back in the food hut. I'll grab it."

"Not that I don't like the view, but being practical."

Some of the leaves are dewy and sizzle as I add the brush to the fire. "Absolutely. We have no idea if they'll come today, tomorrow, or even the day after."

"Right. They might not notice until the cruise ends

tomorrow, and then it's a day and a half to get here from any port."

I kneel by the fire, watching it blaze back to life. "So earliest is this afternoon. Latest would be the day after tomorrow."

"We have plenty of pickles. We should double check everything in the hut."

"And finish the cooked oysters today. We can't afford to get food poisoning out here."

Bailey nods. "Agreed."

We gaze at each other, and a flush comes over her cheeks. "And nakedness inside the shed during the day."

"There won't be satellite spies."

"I don't want to end up starring in a castaway sex tape!"

This makes me laugh. "All right. Sex in the shed."

"It's a date."

She approaches with the sunscreen and smears a bit on my cheeks and nose. "Now go get your shirt on, Mr. Armstrong, or I'll be dragging you to the shed before breakfast."

"Ms. Johansson, you sure are impertinent in the mornings. I might have to take this up with HR."

She reaches forward and grabs me by the groin. "I wouldn't go to HR when I have you by the balls."

She's too close not to kiss. I draw her against me. "I have to confess I had a little fantasy about never being rescued."

Her bright eyes meet mine. "Then that makes two of us."

27

BAILEY

By the end of day two on the island, we have a decent domestic situation.

Rhett has amassed a pile of limbs to keep the fire going. I've figured out a way to daisy chain the life jackets together to create a surprisingly sturdy mattress for inside the shed.

We are definitely tired of sand and the salty grit that comes from washing off in the ocean.

The water was perfectly drinkable, but we spent some time boiling and cooling it anyway, refilling the plastic bags that once held ice.

And our margaritas aren't slushy or even on the rocks anymore, but by dinner, we have made due with a combination of the mix packet, water, and pickle juice.

As the sun sets with no sign of a rescue today, all the oysters gone, Rhett sits by the fire with a hammer, a screwdriver, and two coconuts we found at the base of the trees when we took a short walk inside the tree line.

"Look at us, being hunter-gatherers," I tell him as he

angles the screwdriver on the edge of the outer shell and picks up the hammer.

"Don't congratulate me yet. This husk looks pretty impenetrable."

I sip a margarita from a paper cup while he practices his swing. Now that the sun is down, his shirt is off and I very much enjoy the play of the firelight on his chest and arms as he prepares to smash into the coconut.

"Here goes nothing." He lifts the hammer and brings it down hard on the end of the screwdriver.

The coconut shoots out from under it and rolls across the sand.

"Coconut 1, Rhett 0," I say.

He shakes his head. "This is probably a lost cause."

"No saw or anything?"

"Nope. The tools were focused on repairing the equipment."

"Hmmm." I take another sip. The wind rushes through the palm trees, making a rustling sound in the fronds that has already become familiar. The roar of the waves is ever-present.

I miss having a normal shower. Soap. Doom-scrolling social media rants, one of my guilty pleasures.

But it's nice here, at least so far. I'm hungry, mainly because I couldn't stomach another pickle today. But the margaritas take the edge off.

Rhett scoops up the coconut for another go at it.

This time when the husk shoots across the sand, bouncing off a kayak, I can't help but laugh. "Should I try?"

He holds out the hammer. "Absolutely."

I wonder how I can improve upon his technique. I could ask him to hold the coconut, but accidentally smashing his finger would impact my enjoyment of the evening later. And a wild swing could cause a concussion.

But I do have an idea.

I dig a hole in the sand and place the coconut down in it. I pack it tight so that there isn't any space for the coconut to move.

I run my hand across the hairy surface, looking for any weak spots. I feel a small dent.

I fit the flat end of the screwdriver into that dent and accept the hammer from Rhett.

"What do I get if I'm the one to defeat the coconut?" I ask.

"You mean other than coconut in your margarita?"

"Mmmm hmmm."

"Three orgasms in a row."

I nearly drop my hammer. "Two nearly killed me."

He leans forward to kiss my forehead. "Then let's aim for oblivion."

"Now it's on," I tell the coconut.

I practice like Rhett did, lifting and lowering my hammer for the swing to ensure a solid strike.

"Here it goes." I raise my arm and bring it down so fast that I almost hear the air whistle.

The screwdriver sinks into the husk.

"Hey!" I set the hammer down and peer down at it. "Did I breach its defenses?"

Rhett grasps the screwdriver handle. "Maybe we can wiggle it back and forth to get it to crack."

"I don't think that husk is going to crack."

The moment Rhett starts to move the screwdriver, the coconut works loose from the sand. Soon he's holding it in the air like the world's hairiest lollipop.

"Any other ideas?" he asks.

"Bury it again. Strike it harder." I start digging in the sand. I've got a taste for coconut water now.

When the coconut is back in the sand, Rhett takes the hammer. Before he uses it, he says, "And what do I get if I crack it?"

The margarita is in full force. I whip off my bikini top and drop it in the sand. "These coconuts are all yours."

He takes them in, as if pondering whether to bother with the real coconut.

I point to the screwdriver. "Now focus."

"How am I supposed to do that with such a gorgeous view?"

I cross my arms over my chest. "Better?"

He sighs. "I'm going to devour those later."

"Tipped with coconut water."

He sets the hammer on the sand. "Now I think I could hammer this thing with my dick."

I almost fall backwards, the laughter comes at me so fast. "Rhett!"

I could never have imagined a conversation like this during all those stressful days of filing reports and figuring out how to avoid setting him off.

But here I am, topless, talking about his cock.

"Just try, Mister Hammerhead!"

He tilts his head to assess me. "I could use some motivation."

I throw my arms wide. "Like this?"

"Exactly." He picks up the hammer. "I'm getting that coconut water."

He lifts his arm and brings it down in one smooth strike onto the end of the screwdriver.

The coconut cracks, and the screwdriver falls out.

I lean forward. "Hey! Don't lose the water!"

Rhett lifts it from the dirt. "Let's see what we've got. Open wide."

I lean back and open my mouth.

Rhett upturns the coconut and a thin stream of water falls into my mouth.

It's cool and delicious. I've never tasted anything so good.

When I swallow, Rhett dribbles more of the water over my skin.

"I'm going to take mine like this."

He buries the coconut in the sand so it won't fall over and leak.

Then his mouth follows the trail of the water.

And our night begins.

28

RHETT

A sound startles me awake during the night.

Instinctively, I draw Bailey closer to my chest. We originally slept in the shed, but the lack of breeze quickly became stifling, so we moved our makeshift mattress out by the fire.

It's down to embers, and the very first hint of dawn shows as a blue haze over the ocean.

But then I sit up. There's a shadow on the water. A big one.

It's the cruise ship.

It's back.

I shake Bailey awake. We had originally agreed not to sleep naked because of this very possibility, but when our second night went about like the first, we ended up scattering our bathing suits again.

I reach for her white cover-up and drape it over her. "The ship is out in the water."

She murmurs something unintelligible and tries to snuggle back in, but I shake her shoulder. "We might want to get dressed. They're probably going to boat here any minute."

This snaps her awake. "What do you mean, they?"

I point to the ocean. "I heard something that woke me, and I see the shape of the ship."

She holds her cover-up to her chest as she scrambles for her bathing suit. "Is it ours? Can you tell?"

"No. It's too dark still. But it's the right size and shape."

As I slide on my shorts, she asks, "What do you think you heard?" She's managed to get her bottoms on and faces away from the ocean as she fastens her top.

"I don't know. Obviously, something my subconscious knew was not any of the usual sounds."

"Funny how fast you can assimilate to anything." She ties her wrap over her suit and slides on her flip-flops.

I grab my shirt and shoes, and we slowly head toward the shore.

"I see a little boat, I think," Bailey says. "Do you see it?"

I peer into the murky water and finally make out the shadow of a tiny boat, much smaller than the one we came in on, easing toward the shore. Lights wink in and out as it moves through the waves.

Bailey stands on tiptoe as if that will help her see better. "I guess they're just scouting, because that's an awful small boat to get us."

It isn't safe for us to approach the broken dock in the half-dark, so we wait on the shore. The lights on the boat grow brighter as it nears the beach, and I make out the forms of two people on board.

"Still no way to know who they are," Bailey says.

"It will be crew. Nobody from the company."

She glances behind us.

I know exactly what she's thinking. Our idyllic solitude has come to an end.

The sun continues to rise, giving enough light that we can make out a cap on one of the two heads.

Bailey squints out over the water. "I'm pretty sure that's the driver who brought us out on the small boat. I sat next to him."

She might be right, although I don't remember the man clearly. "You ready to go back to the real world?"

She sighs. "I guess we don't have a choice."

The distance is greater than it appears, and eventually we sit in the sand to wait for them to arrive. The sun rises quickly, and it becomes easy to make out both the cruise ship and the small boat slowly motoring toward us in the waves.

"At least they aren't having to use oars," Bailey says.

"It's a small vessel for that distance. They have to be fighting the waves."

"Actually, we will fight them to get back out. The waves go toward the shore."

I chuckle. Bailey always has to be right.

She bumps her shoulder against mine. "Sorry. Force of habit. Correcting you was one of my favorite pastimes."

"I remember."

"What are we going to do from here?" she asks.

"Take it one step at a time, I guess."

When the boat is within shouting distance, we both stand up again. The driver in front waves at us. He's short and stocky, and Bailey is right. He's the same driver who brought us to the island as a group.

A tall, lean man in back adjusts the motor so the propellers are level with the stern as they get into the shallows.

We wade out to meet them.

The man in the cap speaks first. "Rhett Armstrong? Bailey Johansson?" He grins at Bailey. "I remember you."

"I might be more trouble than I'm worth," she says.

"Could be," he says with a grin.

"Is that our ship?" I ask.

"It is. We circled back." The two men drag the boat up onto the beach as we follow along.

The man in the cap turns to look us over. "I'm Chief Officer Mory. You both seem well. Are you sick? Dehydrated? It's been two days."

"We built a fire to boil water," I tell him. "We found a few things to tide us over."

"Good." He turns to the taller man with a short-clipped gray beard. "This is Dr. Jarvis, the attending physician for our cruises. Do you mind if he checks you out?"

Bailey and I glance at each other. "Sure," I say. "Bailey has a cut on her arm, but we found the first aid kit."

The four of us walk back to the fire. Dr. Jarvis listens to Bailey's breathing and checks her pupils. He peels back the gauze. "We'll treat this once we're back on board."

"Are we riding back with you to the ship?" I ask.

"No choice. We can't bring anything bigger with the dock as it is," Mory says. "Nobody will be visiting this island for quite a while. You're lucky you're okay. We didn't know what we'd find."

"We took cover in the hut," I say.

Dr. Jarvis turns to it. "The one without a roof?"

"Better than the one that totally collapsed." I gesture to the pile of bamboo that once housed the bathrooms.

Mory shakes his head. "This was a colossal oversight. We will be reviewing our evacuation procedures to ensure we account for all passengers."

"That's good to hear." While the doctor asks me to breathe deeply, Bailey heads into the shed to gather her things. She's hanging onto one of our towels. A souvenir, I guess.

"I'm going to take a few pictures," Mory says. "Document the damage. Then we'll head back."

Dr. Jarvis, Bailey, and I walk to the boat while Mory wanders the beach, snapping shots with his phone.

It's a tight fit, but we squeeze on the two seats as Mory pushes the small boat out into the waters. Dr. Jarvis drops the motor back into the sea once we're deep enough.

Gradually, the ship grows closer and closer.

Several people wait on the side dock where the larger boat is moored to the yacht.

A few are in Blue Sapphire uniforms, but I also

recognize Sarah and her husband Caleb. Gloria stands nearby, her hands tightly clasped together.

When we're in earshot, Sarah calls out, "What the hell, Rhett! I knew you were sick of us, but seriously!"

I reach over to squeeze Bailey's hand, then realize this is going to be new to the staff. Everyone aboard that ship knows I fired her. That she sneaked onto the cruise. They will expect that we've been at each other's throats the whole time.

Probably no one could have predicted what actually happened on that island.

It already feels like a far-off dream.

We approach the open side of the ship, and Mory tosses the lead line to the crew. Within seconds, we are up against the dock, and the crew members reach for Bailey to help her out.

"My word," Gloria says. "I thought you were both dead."

Bailey turns to me as I step onto the ship, her eyebrows raised. She knows our rescue will be a big deal.

I try to downplay what happened. "It was just a bonus experience," I tell Gloria. "Only available for the boss."

"And stowaways," Bailey adds.

But as everyone watches us, I can see her changing. The presence of people we know, who have opinions about our histories, who might be making judgments about our situation, has altered the easy camaraderie from the island.

"I was so damn worried," Sarah says. "When you wouldn't answer the door, then you didn't show up in the Bahamas, I insisted we go back and check your room."

So, she was the one to figure it out.

I keep an eye on Bailey, who seems to be shrinking in on herself. "Thanks," I say. "Without you, we would've been there another day at least."

"The entire staff voted to come back here rather than stay in port," Gloria says.

Did they? This will definitely be the talk of the cruise.

We have a long journey home. This delay will add an extra day to the trip. And another day we're not at work. Before I can ask the question, Gloria jumps in, "Yes, I already arranged for the temps to come back on Monday since we won't return on time. The satellite feed is back up and everything is fine."

"I see, thank you."

"And we delayed the formal dinner and casino night. Nobody was up for it with you gone." Gloria frowns. "The ship was well appointed even for an extra day, so we had a burger night."

Mory pats my shoulder. "We have it handled, and there will be no additional charges for the extra night. Now, I'm sure Dr. Jarvis wants to look at Miss Johansson's arm, and it wouldn't be a bad idea for both of you to head to the sick bay to be sure you're all right."

"Please come down to the pool when you're situated," Sarah says. "I need to be certain that you're fine."

"Me, too," Gloria says. "There will be no more holing up in your room with paperwork."

I lift my hands in defeat. "All right, all right." I turn

to Mory. "And I'm not holding Blue Sapphire liable for any of this. Bailey and I were way off the beaten path when that storm hit. It was our own fault we got stuck there."

"That's nice and all," Mory says, "but there should've been a headcount before we left the area, storm or no storm."

I move toward Bailey, but she takes a step away, a movement that does not go unnoticed by Gloria.

"If it's all right, Mr. Armstrong, I'll accompany Bailey to the doctor. Perhaps you can come along a while later. Give her some privacy and a break from you."

I want to see how Bailey feels about that, but her eyes are on the floor. "Of course," I say.

Clearly Bailey needs some space. I will give it to her.

And just like that, we're separated.

Bailey leaves with Gloria. I'm left with my VP of operations and the ship's crew.

And I have no idea where I stand with anyone.

29

BAILEY

Rhett looks concerned as I walk away, but I can't do anything about that. The weight of everyone watching me, maybe even guessing what happened on the island, is heavy on me. I want to disappear.

The sick bay is level with the dock down a maze of hallways that include offices and what appear to be smaller rooms for the crew.

Dr. Jarvis gestures for me to hop onto an exam table and lifts my arm. "I know you'll want a shower shortly, so how about I come see you in about an hour and redress this? It doesn't look infected, but let's be cautious. When was your last tetanus shot?"

"I'm not sure."

"Well, I can't remedy that here, but you get yourself updated. I'd follow up with your regular doctor when you get home."

That will be hard to do, and expensive, given I don't currently have health insurance. "But it looks all right? It doesn't hurt."

"It looks fine."

Good enough for me.

He looks in my ear and throat. He listens to me breathe again. "The sunburn doesn't look too bad."

"I've had much worse."

He steps back and watches me with quiet patience. "Is everything else all right?"

I don't know what he means. Is he asking me about what might have happened with Rhett? "I'm great. Just dirty and ready for a change of clothes."

He nods. "You're lucky, Bailey. Not everyone gets left on an island in a storm and lives to tell the tale."

I hop down from the exam table. "Thanks."

Gloria is waiting for me out in the hall. "Do you have your room key?"

"It's in my bag."

"I'll come along and make sure it works."

There's no reason it wouldn't, but it seems I'm not going to shake her, even if I want to be alone for a moment.

Walking next to her, it feels obvious that I spent two days banging her boss.

We're heading up the stairs before she finally spills what's on her mind. "Are you considering legal action against Blue Sapphire and Dougherty?"

I pause on a step. "Why would I do that?"

She stops a few stairs down from me. "Because of what happened. I was the one who suggested you find a quiet place while I spoke to Rhett."

Now I get it. Gloria feels responsible for me getting

left behind. I resume my journey up the steps. "It's fine. What was the evacuation like?"

She follows. "Chaotic. The first group went before the storm, but it started raining while we waited for the second trip and some people panicked."

I try not to smile, imagining Viola dashing around like the sky was falling. "So nobody was checking who was on the boats."

"It was a little hard with two rounds. By the time I made it back on the second trip, the water was choppy, and people were throwing up on the yacht."

Eew. I'm glad I missed that part.

Gloria grimaces, like she's remembering the carnage. "With some sick, some in their rooms, it was hard to take a headcount."

"I bet."

"And then we were sailing away. Naturally I knocked on Rhett's door, but his failure to answer didn't mean anything."

"Not until you got to port."

"Sarah came to me with her concern because she hadn't seen him and had gone to his room several times. We got the crew to open the door."

"Did anyone check mine?"

Her lips pinch.

That's what I thought.

We make it to my floor, and I head down the hall.

Gloria keeps up. "Will you file a suit?" she asks. "I would like Mr. Armstrong to be prepared to handle it."

I pull the keycard from my bag. Sand sprinkles onto

the floor. I guess I have another souvenir from the island, besides the towel I pilfered.

"I'll speak to Rhett about it myself," I tell her, no longer wanting to talk to her or pretty much anybody. I guess I'm lucky Rhett got stuck with me, or maybe I'd have been on the island all alone for the rest of my natural life. "Thank you for your *concern*."

The lock beeps and the door pops open. I give Gloria a nod and step inside, shutting the door firmly.

I lean against it. My room is unchanged. My pajama shorts and top are on the bed, although folded up on the corner. The crew must have come in at some point and made it up.

Interesting. I suppose they didn't report my room being unused. Probably people room-hop on these cruises all the time, and it's nothing they haven't seen before.

Even so, that's strike two for anyone caring that I went missing.

Suddenly, I'm bone-tired. I set my bag on the desk in a cascade of sand.

This makes me laugh. Why not keep it? I take a moment to collect it into one of the crystal glasses.

What a wild two days. Sun, surf, and sex.

As I head to the bathroom, there's a knock at the door. Dr. Jarvis already?

I peer through the peephole.

It's a crew member with a tray.

Food. *Yes.*

I eagerly open the door.

"Hello, ma'am. I've brought you a wide selection of

items in case you are hungry after your ordeal. Let us know if you want anything at all. Our chef will make whatever you like."

He sets the tray on the desk. "Can I assist you with anything else?"

"No. Thank you."

When he's gone, I try to decide, shower or food first?

But when I lift the metal dome from a plate of eggs, bacon, sausage, and hash browns, I literally can't stop myself. I shove food in my mouth so fast that I almost choke.

Finally, I back away, afraid I'll be sick if I eat any more.

In the shower, I let the warm water fall over me, and only then do I allow myself to revisit the moments on the island with Rhett.

Sex in the water. By the fire. On our makeshift mattress.

His face. His arms. His chest. His laugh.

When I close my eyes, every vision is of him. I clutch the silver bar on the wall, trying not to cry. I feel like a piece of me got left behind on that beach.

And it's silly. I can go to him. He won't hate me now.

But I'm afraid.

I'm afraid that I will look at him and he will look at me, and it won't be the same. That the intensity of what happened in those two days was only part of the experi-ence of being left behind, caught in a storm, left to fend for ourselves.

I've never deserved someone like Rhett Armstrong.

I've never deserved a job like I had. I've never earned anything, other than maybe my degree.

The only way someone like me gets a man like Rhett is when there is literally no competition.

Like on an island in a storm.

And now we're going home.

30

———

RHETT

I have to make an appearance before my staff. They need to see me after leaving me behind.

I eat a few bites of the breakfast provided on a tray and take a shower. Then it's into fresh swim trunks and a T-shirt to look casual and relaxed for the last day of the cruise. I told Sarah to move forward with the formal evening tonight. We should celebrate.

Dr. Jarvis stops by right as I'm about to leave, his hands rubbing his short gray beard. "How are you feeling?"

I step back to let him inside the room. "I feel all right. Food went down fine. The shower was a huge relief."

"I bet." He takes me in. "You look good. Things to watch for would be any intestinal trouble. A cough. Did you get sunburned?"

I hold out my arms. "Maybe a little. But nothing too bad."

"All right." He claps my back. "My number is in the directory. Call if you have any concerns."

He's about to go, but I say, "How was Bailey?"

"Seemed fine."

"And her arm?"

"No sign of infection. I'll check her again before you all disembark in the morning."

"Good." I hesitate. "And did she seem all right, otherwise?"

His bushy gray eyebrows lift. "What do you mean?"

"Emotionally. She was okay?"

Dr. Jarvis brushes his beard with the back of his knuckles. "She might have been subdued. Hard to say, since I don't know her. But not distraught. You might check in on her, though. Tough thing, getting stranded like that."

Now he's the one who hesitates. "Did something happen we should know about?"

"No, no. We were good together." I quickly add, "Gathering firewood, things like that." I'm rambling.

Dr. Jarvis watches me for a moment. "Well, if you have something you need to let me know about, give me a call." He waits a beat longer. "All right then."

This time, I open the door and let him go. I don't know what I was after. Maybe seeing if Bailey was feeling regret? Upset?

If she was, she hid it, at least for Dr. Jarvis.

And Gloria, of course. I don't think Bailey would let Gloria see anything she was feeling.

I tuck the keycard into my pocket and head down the hall. Dr. Jarvis is still walking away, whistling.

I don't know which room is Bailey's, and our phones don't have a signal on the water for me to contact her. I'll have to ask the crew where she is. But for now, I have to parade myself on the deck.

When I arrive at the pool, a great cheer goes up.

That was unexpected.

Then, I'm surrounded. Everyone wants to shake my hand and clap me on the back, like I'm a celebrity or a hero.

"Hell of a thing, Rhett."

"You don't look like you got stranded on a deserted island!"

"Did you find a way to work, anyway?"

"Did you have to eat raw fish to survive?"

No one asks about Bailey, but I catch Gloria watching me from a chair near the hot tub. She doesn't look pleased, and I wonder if Bailey told her anything. Surely our relationship on the beach is of no concern to HR.

Or is it?

And what did Bailey say?

The second person I notice is Viola. She glowers at me from the edge of the pool, even though she's got some young buck I don't recognize staring down her cleavage like it's a magic mirror.

I would like very much to glower back, now that I know what she did to Bailey, but I have appearances to keep up at the moment. Viola will get her due all in good time.

I shake hands and accept a beer that is fetched for

me. I'm tempted to drink the whole thing in one chug. *That* would get the party started.

But I'm already stiffening up, hardening under the pressure of being the boss. They need me to be something I'm not. Real Rhett isn't the right guy for the job.

What boss would compromise his former assistant when she couldn't even go for help if she wanted?

In the light of day, among all the people whose livelihoods depend on me, I realize how bad this looks. Me, all over a woman I fired. Taking advantage of her, of our isolation.

My palms start to sweat. I make an excuse and head to the rail, hoping the wind and the view will distract me.

Sarah appears. "I'd keep those coming if I were you," she says, gesturing at the beer bottle. "I would have fallen plumb apart if I got stuck on an island with anybody, must less someone I dismissed."

I fix my gaze firmly on the water. "We're all right. I need to look at the dailies. We did have a conversation about the marketing debacle. I got some information I need to check into."

Sarah turns to me. "What sort of information?"

"Another employee who may have faked some documents."

"Rhett! That's serious. I've never worked anywhere that had issues like this."

Right. Because probably at her last company, the boss wasn't the owner's incompetent nephew who got hired purely based on his name and not a whit for his ability to do the job.

Sarah is clearly distressed. "Maybe we need an external audit."

I put on my best authoritative voice. It's well practiced. "Let me follow the trail of paperwork. It's in my room. It was always going to be my priority."

Sarah braces her elbows on the rail. "Whatever you say, Rhett. But if this mess leaks to the clients, we'll lose billing."

I know it, but I take a swig of the beer and decide not to answer.

We stand there, watching the cut of the water where the yacht sluices through the waves. I want to find Bailey, see where we are with all that.

Finally, I push away. "I'll see you and Caleb at dinner?"

"Of course." Her gaze stays on me, her hair blowing in every direction. "You sure you're all right?"

"Totally. Completely. Don't worry about a thing." I give her a nod and head for the closest crew member. I'm definitely not going to ask Gloria to take me to Bailey.

The woman in the blue uniform knows who I am. She agrees to look up Bailey's room number and take me there.

I guess that's one thing that's good about being the boss—generally, I get what I want, whether I deserve it or not.

31

BAILEY

The knock at the door is clearly Rhett. It's got too much authority, like he's telling you to open up or face the consequences.

Old Rhett. The one I worked for.

Not the one on the beach, the lines crinkling around his eyes as we poured margaritas.

I don't even want to open it, honestly. To have to face boorish Rhett after having the other version feels exhausting. I'm not up for it.

But then he taps more lightly. "Bailey?" His voice is plaintive, like he's worried.

I tuck the glass of sand I've collected behind a lamp. I don't want him to think I'm being sentimental about our time on the island.

Even if I am.

When I open the door, a hundred emotions wash over me as I look at him standing in the hallway.

His sea-green T-shirt emphasizes how dark his hair

is. It fits perfectly over his chest, which I can picture without even closing my eyes, as if I had X-ray vision.

A pair of yellow board shorts complements it perfectly and makes his tan pop. He's wearing flip-flops and there are those perfect toes, now clear of sand.

I'm struck by his hands most of all. I don't think I paid enough attention to them when we worked together. But I know where they've been. On me. Inside me. A glow forms low in my belly.

He waits me out, his eyes on me. Maybe he's doing the same thing, re-categorizing, remembering.

I assumed I'd see him before the day ended, so I put on a white sundress with a stretchy top and straps that tie in a bow on my shoulders.

Without a bra, it's a little revealing, and I know exactly when his gaze falls there, my nipples tightening in response.

I wasn't sure how he'd be when we saw each other again, but now it's clear. The attraction hasn't changed.

I step back to let him in and close the door.

My back presses against the cool surface as I lean on it. He turns to wait me out, his expression uncertain.

It feels like there's a lot to say about where we've been, where we're going, but in true Bailey fashion, I blurt out, "I'm not wearing panties."

And then he's on me, pushing me against the door, his hands lifting my skirt as if to verify my claim.

I'm wet, so wet, almost from the moment I realized the knock on the door had to be his.

His mouth takes mine, and he's so familiar, and I'm so relieved that my eyes smart with emotion.

His hands move up my thighs until his thumbs press into me.

I gasp against his mouth.

The circular motion makes me tingle all over. I clutch his neck, my legs giving out.

He swings me up into his arms and carries me to the narrow bed. One hand returns to where he was, his gaze on my face as he touches me.

It's different here, more cushioned and secure than in the sand and unknown night. I close my eyes, an arm thrown over my forehead.

His fingers work me, drawing out the need. Lightning bolts of pleasure dart up my body.

Then he spreads my knees wider and his warm mouth replaces his fingers. His hair tickles my exposed belly, and I look down.

My white dress is bunched at my waist. I can only see the top of his head. I reach down to thread my fingers through his hair.

He sucks hard, and I cry out. Then I clap my hand over my mouth. I don't know who my neighbors are, but I definitely can't be shouting the boss's name.

Rhett adds fingers to increase the intensity. I hold onto his hair with one hand and the sheets with the other—so much better than sand—and begin that climb. My muscles clench. I stare up at the fancy ceiling tiles. I didn't expect to be seeing them like this.

Then all those thoughts are blown out by the rhythmic pulsing down below.

He did this to me. The first time. Then again and again. Only him.

I try to be aware of what I'm saying, how loud I might be. But the bed tilts, like the ship is capsizing. I hang on for dear life as my body thrums with the waves inside me, making everything slide off kilter.

I'm still sideways as Rhett kisses his way up my belly, moving the dress out of his way as he goes. I realize it's only me going sideways. My body. My world. The ship is fine.

Only as he lifts me to tug the dress over my head do I start to feel like the world has righted itself.

I sink onto the sheets, looking up at him.

"Beds are better," he says, and he's so like himself from the beach, so different from that strident knock, that I have to laugh.

"They are." I draw him down to me, his cotton clothes against my bare body. I want to hold onto this moment, hold onto him.

We're going to be all right.

After a moment, he presses his lips against my cheek and starts working his way down again. "Now I get the less gritty version," he says, then closes his mouth on a breast.

I arch to him, happy and sated and ready for more, all at the same time.

He breaks away to get rid of his shirt.

I touch everything I got to know on the island. The indention in the center of his chest. The lines between the muscles of his abs.

His swim trunks are loose enough to contain what's down there, but I swiftly untie them and push the shorts down.

There he is.

I hold him, hot and hard. I was so worried, but here we are, back where we were. It was never the time or the place.

It was a misunderstanding that kept us apart.

And now nothing does.

I draw him down and into me.

He fills my body and I gasp, enjoying the smooth feel of our skin without the humidity and sand.

"We're so clean!" I have to say.

Rhett chuckles in my ear, and I swear I will never tire of that sound.

He moves inside me with a leisurely pace that's so different from our frantic previous two days.

His gaze meets mine and the connection locks. I find myself paying tight attention to his face, to each tiny detail of his expression.

His eyes soften as he braces himself over me on his elbows.

We take our time, moving together, and I wrap my legs around his waist.

"Bailey," he says, and it's a whisper, reverent, like a prayer.

"Rhett." I match him, my voice catching.

We're safe. No wondering when the boat will come, what we will eat, worrying about keeping the fire going.

It shows in how we relax into each other, savoring the feel of our bodies, the comfort of the bed, the protection from the elements.

He pushes my hair from my forehead and plants a

soft kiss above my eyebrow. The pleasure of his movements unfurls slowly, like a flower blooming.

Then the fire kicks in, and our breathing speeds up. Rhett grasps my head and moves with more deliberation.

I want him so deep, so hard. I tighten my legs on his hips.

He thrusts powerfully inside me, making me gasp.

I clutch his shoulders, feeling reality slip again.

This one is different, so far down, so broad and wide. When the tightening begins, it takes over more of my body. My moan is low and guttural, from my very center.

Rhett keeps the pace hard and fast, holding me from beneath my shoulders to keep me steady.

My body clenches, and I have to hold back the volume of my cries.

Rhett buries his face in my hair and says my name, "Bailey, Bailey, Bailey," over and over again.

We hang onto each other, lashed together like a boat crew in a storm.

He pulses into me, warm and wet and comforting.

We hold still a while longer, letting the relief and emotion wash over us.

Then he slides to the side, drawing a sheet over us as he pulls me to his chest.

We're quiet a while longer, listening to the sounds of the boat. The vessel creaks as it carves its way through the water. The footsteps of people walking on the floor above are a distant thud, and the waves splash endlessly against the hull.

Rhett kisses my hair above my ear. "Are we going to go out there as a couple or would you like to stay private?"

I consider his question. "What do you think?"

"I think I've made you miserable enough with my bad decisions. I will let you call the shots on this."

I snuggle into his neck. "We have all the time in the world to be public. Let's be private a little while longer."

"Okay." He draws me more securely against him, and this time when we sleep, it's the heavy slumber of security, safety, and contentment.

32

RHETT

I wake up in late afternoon, the sun bright in the window.

Bailey stirs, then looks up at me sleepily. "I dreamed we were back on the island, only with a good bed."

I lift her hand to kiss her wrist. "That would definitely have improved things."

She stretches, and I admire everything about her as the sheet falls away. She shakes her head. "We are so wild together. Or are you always like this?"

"Not in the least."

She likes this answer. "So what is on our agenda now that we're rescued?"

"They moved the formal dinner to tonight. Nobody wanted to do it last night since we were missing."

"*You* were missing," she corrects. "Gloria says they never checked my cabin."

"I have quite a few words to say to my staff."

"Your staff. It must be nice being the boss. Knowing

your place. Feeling confident in your position." She snuggles back into my chest.

I wonder if I should tell her how far off the mark she is. That I'm only here due to my uncle's generosity. But before I can correct her, she says, "You know, it's the worst having aspirations outside of how you grew up."

"You did, I take it?"

"I did. The whole politics angle. Not to be a politician, of course. But to be part of it. In the capitol. Watching it all happen. Researching. Helping."

She mentioned something about this before. "But you didn't."

"Couldn't. All the internships went to people who had connections. Family. Business partners. Until I tried to break into it, I had no idea how much of it was rigged. Sure, some people worked hard and broke in anyway, but they were exceptions. Everyone liked to point to them as if to say, 'See, you can do it, too.' But I couldn't. Breaking in without someone giving you a leg up was like winning the lottery."

My stomach turns. She's talking about exactly the situation I'm in. No one else has a shot at my job because it was made solely for me.

"I think you would have made an excellent senator's assistant."

She nips at my shoulder. "I would have. Are you about to go give a speech I didn't write?"

I chuckle even though I'm not feeling the lightness of it. "I'm sure it will be vastly inferior to the one you would have prepared."

"How long do you have?"

I glance at the clock on the narrow shelf. "Not much time. In fact, I better get to my cabin to shower and dress."

She stays in bed as I pull away. "I don't think I'm going to go," she says. "I'm not up for facing everyone yet."

"That's fine. All in good time." I lean down to kiss her again. "I'll be back as soon as I can possibly escape."

"Okay." Her gaze follows me as I gather my clothes. "I'll be waiting."

When I arrive at the dining room, straightening the tie to my tux, Gloria is waiting outside the door. "You're on as soon as you're ready." She takes over fixing my bowtie. "If you aren't up for giving a speech after your ordeal, we can make excuses."

"I'm fine."

She steps away. "The cards to the speech you wrote before we left are on the podium. You might want to add a line or two about the island. And stop by your table to say hello. Sarah and her husband are there as well as Matthew from accounting and his wife, along with my husband."

"Got it." I tug at my collar and suddenly flash with the moment I murmured to Bailey that we should have a naked day on the island. Lots better than this monkey suit.

But outwardly, I nod and smile at the employees I pass, already seated at their tables with salads and wine.

I pause near the front to greet Sarah and Matthew.

Then it's to the podium.

A crew member hurries forward to test the microphone. I glance through the cards, noting a line I can alter to mention the island escapade.

This will be fine.

"It's all yours," the woman says and steps off to the side.

I don't mind speeches. I have to stand in boardrooms all the time and give presentations.

But looking out on the room full of my employees today feels different. They're all leaning into each other, whispering and glancing my way. I feel like a fish out of water, gulping for air.

I set my cards down. It might be better to go off the cuff.

"Hello, everyone. Welcome to the final dinner of our company cruise. It looks a far cry better than leftover oysters and a bucket of pickles, which is what I lived on yesterday."

Everyone laughs, and the whispering stops completely. I have their attention.

"One thing being stranded on an island will teach you is that only a few things are important. Clean water. Avoiding injury. Staying out of the sun. During my time there, I got a crash course in prioritization. It's one of the lessons I will take back with me to Dougherty." On the fly, I decide, "So naturally no one is expected to go in tomorrow even though we will dock early in the morning. We will let the temps handle it. It's more important we recover from this adventure, me included."

A wave of cheers rises.

From there, I mostly do the speech as intended. It's brief, and everyone claps when appropriate. It's a good transition from the wildness of my rescue back to business.

Now to see how quickly I can eat dinner and get back to Bailey.

I'm about to head to my table when I see her.

My breath catches.

She has entered through the rear doors. She wears a sparkling red dress, and her chestnut hair streaked with purple is pulled into a sweeping updo fastened with a rhinestone clasp.

The dress is strapless, showing off a tan, no doubt augmented by our days on the island. It has a heart-shaped top, dipping between those delicious breasts I can easily picture.

She glances around, looking for an empty seat.

There's one at my table, since I'm a single with three couples.

But she said we would stay private, and she calls the shots.

I realize I'm standing, dumbstruck, in front of the entire company. A few people turn to see what has caught my attention.

The whispering resumes.

She's spotted a table with two couples from mainte-nance. Peter stands and pulls out a chair for her. The woman next to him, presumably his wife, takes Bailey's hand in both of hers, clearly glad to see her.

I'm still staring.

"Rhett?" It's Gloria, come to my rescue. "Let's have a seat."

But that's the moment Bailey glances around, her gaze directly meeting mine this time. She watches me, then her hand lifts and she gestures for me to come to her.

I walk away from Gloria and the table with my VP of operations and head of accounting, and glide toward her as if pulled by a string.

The room is quiet, watching as I approach her table.

Bailey smiles and tugs out the empty chair to her right. "Peter, Bea, Harry, Suni, I'm sure Rhett Armstrong needs no introduction."

The four of them murmur greetings, trying to contain their shock.

Then I sit down, almost in a daze, and Bailey takes my hand.

"We thought you all should be the first to know that I'll be back at the company next week, and that Rhett and I will be striking the fraternization rule from the employee handbook, not that it was ever enforced."

"How lovely," Bea says. "I always thought the two of you would be good together."

"Must have been an interesting two days on the island," Griswold says, patting his long bushy beard with his linen napkin.

Bea elbows him hard enough that he lets out a sudden, "Ooof."

Harry and Suni try to bite back smiles.

"Rhett was a perfect gentleman," Bailey says. "We worked out all our differences that led to my firing, and realized what a great team we make."

"We're glad you made it through all right," Bea says, shifting her bright pink boa from her shoulders to her elbows to avoid getting feathers in her salad. She lifts her wine glass. "Here's to good things coming from difficult circumstances."

They all clink their glasses. I pick up the extra water glass to tap with them.

A server quickly brings me and Bailey salads and offers us wine.

The conversation moves on to the wild ride in the storm on the boat as if nothing unexpected has been revealed.

Bailey leans close to my ear. "I decided the island was enough private time. Let's get in there and find us some proof."

I lift her hand to my lips. "I'm happy to let you lead the way."

33

———

BAILEY

R hett and I were *supposed* to look at the dailies when we got in from the formal dinner.

We went to his room, which is much bigger and fancier than mine, and we even opened one of the binders Gloria prepared for him.

But then he couldn't take his hands off my red dress.

Then I wasn't *wearing* the red dress.

And the binders were forgotten.

We stayed together all night, then in the morning we pack his room, then mine, and leave the boat side-by-side.

No one is expected to go to work today, so the mood is jovial as we all walk to our cars.

Rhett loads my suitcases into the back of my pride and joy, a red Mini Cooper with a stripe down the middle. When he closes the hatch, he leans against the back of the car. "So, what now?"

I'm not sure if he means right this minute, or the

future of our relationship, or what how we will manage my return to work.

"That's a big question," I say.

"Nobody's at the office today other than a few temps," he says.

Now we're talking. "Are you suggesting we break in your office?"

He chuckles low and sexy. "Now that's a great idea. But I was thinking more about doing some sleuthing while no one's around, before anyone can tamper with any data."

"You mean Viola."

"For starters."

"Okay, let's do it. I'll drop off my suitcases and check on Maxwell, and I'll meet you at the office in an hour."

"Do I get to meet my rival sometime?" His grin almost knocks me off balance. He really does look like Henry Cavill.

"Certainly. Just don't expect him to sleep with you."

Rhett makes such a horrible face that I have to laugh.

"Come on. We can discuss your relationship with my pussy another time."

He leans down to brush a gentle kiss on my mouth. "We can figure out where we're sleeping tonight over dinner."

That settles both questions, I guess. My body tingles as he opens my car door and waits for me while I slide behind the wheel. "See you at Dougherty."

He nods. "I'll reinstate your passcode on the back entry."

Now that's something. "All right then."

I hum along with every song on the radio. Tunes that never applied to me now make me smile. "You Belong to Me." "Until I Found You."

But when the new Ed Sheeran and Sam Smith song comes on, "Who We Love," I have to pull over into a grocery store parking lot.

Every word seems written just for me. I know it's about harder loves than mine. And mine isn't even love. How can it be, when I absolutely loathed Rhett only three days ago?

But it speaks to me so deeply that I'm weeping. Crying for how hard things got. How much hope I lost. How scared I was in that storm.

By the time the song is over, I feel cried out. Things are good. My job is back. Nothing bad happened with my apartment or my bills. And Rhett is something entirely new to me than he was before.

I wipe my face with a random Kleenex in the console and head to my apartment.

When I open the door, Maxwell sits in the middle of the dining table, eyes narrowed like he's never going to forgive me for leaving him.

And Rhett thought Maxwell was my boyfriend.

I erupt in giggles, making Maxwell more annoyed. He turns around to show me his butt and the twitch of his tail.

"Oh, you silly boy," I tell him and pull out the super

deluxe tuna treats that I save for when I'm trying to woo him. "Come here, my sweet little man."

He holds out for several minutes, and I'm about to put them away again when he hops down from the table and sits at my feet.

"Good boy," I say, and lean down with the treats in my palm.

He gobbles them quickly, then off he goes, tail twitching, not bothering to look behind him.

I roll my bags to my room. The note from the pet sitter tells me that he only threw up once, and that he didn't seem to notice the extra day I was gone.

I check my hair and add a touch more makeup to the quick face I put on with Rhett on the ship this morning.

I was with Rhett this morning!

I think for only a moment about last night, and the afternoon before, and all the times we were together on the island. I press my hand to my chest. That was a lot. I've never been like this. Nobody I've dated has been like Rhett.

It's like we're two butterflies in spring, spinning around each other in a dizzying dance.

My phone buzzes. It's Rhett.

Parking. Come when you like. I'm going to check on the temps.

I should get up there.

I blow a quick kiss to Maxwell, laughing again at Rhett's mistake, and hurry to my car.

When I tap my old code into the security panel at the garage entrance to the building, my body buzzes with victory. I fixed this! I'm back!

More than back. I'm with Rhett!

It's only been two weeks since I last walked these halls, but it feels like a lifetime ago. Other companies also rent space in the building, and it's a normal Monday for them. Workers walk near the front entrance, and the security guard watches people come and go.

I take the elevator up to the fifth floor where Rhett has his office. Dougherty occupies the top two floors of the building.

Since reception is below our floor, I assume the temps will all be down there. This level houses the executives and human resources as well as the small boardroom and the big meeting space for larger company gatherings.

I set my bag on my old desk. It's emptier than I left it, devoid of even the basics of a pencil holder and trays. The computer monitor is dark, not even in the power save mode IT always wants us to remain in.

Rhett's door is partially open. I knock on the outside, then step inside. He's not at his desk but sits at the small meeting table in the front corner, all the binders from the cruise spread in front of him.

I slide onto a chair. "You got started."

"I'm looking at the requisitions Viola brought me that day and matching them up to actual checks that were cut."

I lean over. "What did you find?"

"There aren't any."

I sit up straight. "What do you mean?"

He points at one of the invoices. "This was billed to

the fake company, Anton Archer Services. But there is no actual money transfer in that name."

"Are there any for that amount? Maybe they are under some billing umbrella?" I turn the binder so I can read it.

"Sure, but those are all legitimate bills paid to our usual advertising firm, Langston & Evans. They generate our leads, place ads in industry publications, and do follow-up on cold clients. We've used them since we started."

"Wait." I pull the accounting log printouts toward me. "The billing number is only one digit off. Do you think this was a clerical error?"

"On half a million dollars' worth of requisitions dating over a year?"

"Well, if it auto fills, it would keep auto filling. When was the first one?"

We madly flip through the binders to keep looking.

"August 7 of last year," Rhett says.

"Are there any official billings for Langston & Evans after that?" I run my finger down the column.

"Yes. They have an active account." Rhett stabs his finger at several entries.

"But no money went to Archer. You're sure."

"Someone specifically set up this fake account and changed the numbers on enough requisitions, all signed by you, to set you up."

"So, Viola." I sit back in my chair.

Rhett's scowl is deep, his eyebrows drawn close together. "She was good. Some of these are backdated even though she couldn't have been playing a long game. This sort of error would have been caught in the audit last quarter. These were recent changes."

I flip through all the altered documents. "I don't think Viola has the technical skill or the patience to set this up."

"So someone helped her?"

"Who would have the ability to change all these requisitions without pinging the system with an error?"

"Accounting," Rhett says.

I snap my fingers. "And IT."

"So someone got bamboozled by Viola to do this?"

I shrug. "She's got some pretty persuasive skills." I'd seen it plenty.

Rhett closes the binders. "I'll take Luke in IT aside tomorrow and have him conduct a discreet audit of the code."

"Why Luke when Hammond is the head of the department?"

"Because Luke is happily married, and Hammond is single and could be swayed."

I nod. "I see."

He pulls me onto his lap. "So we have a plan. What was this about breaking in my office?"

I nip his ear. "But Mr. Bossman, what will everyone say?"

He lifts me onto the table and spreads my knees. "They'll say, what a lucky man."

And then I'm lying on my back, and my skirt is around my waist.

Now this is a job I can get into.

34

RHETT

On Tuesday morning, I arrive early, hoping to get to the IT department before Viola can see me and start covering her tracks.

The tech team has a few members who arrive at six to make sure the servers are in good shape before anyone logs in, and a few others who will be the last in the company to leave.

Luke is part of the first wave.

I weave through the sea of cubicles until I get to his. It's right outside Hammond's office, which fortunately is still closed and dark.

Luke spots me and waves. "You're here early."

"There's a matter that needs handling. A delicate one."

Luke spins in his chair to face me. "All right."

There's no other chair in his cube, so I lean against the upholstered wall. He has Dilbert cartoons pinned all over the inside, plus a caricature of himself in Dilbert's outfit, only with his red hair and beard.

"I'm not going to Hammond with this, not yet, so I'm looking for some discretion." I watch Luke carefully to gauge his reaction. If something seems off, I will pivot and ask him to pull different logs.

His eyebrows lift, but otherwise, he doesn't show any nervousness or concern. "Okay, not a problem. What did you need?"

I unfurl the pages from the dailies Bailey and I reviewed yesterday. "I need to know who might have made changes to these requisitions and when they did it." I set the pages down.

Luke picks them up. "There should be a simple signature trail on these."

"It's the client ID I'm looking at. For this client." I point to the correct agency, the real one. "We have about half a million in requisitions moved to a new client ID that is one digit off. It appears to be a fictitious company."

Luke shakes his head. "That's quite a feat. Some of these are old. The audit should have caught it."

"Which is why I think it was done recently, probably about two to three weeks ago."

He flips through the pages. "These are completely random dates and numeric values. Did you see any pattern?"

"Only that they were all for Langston & Evans."

Luke types a few commands into his keyboard. "Oh yeah, they are showing way under-billed compared to old years in accounts payable."

"But do a quick look at the payment."

He types again. "Yep. Checks were cut to them. Not

to this Anton Archer outfit. I don't show any money flowing to them."

"Exactly. Someone wanted it to temporarily appear that someone was funneling money to Archer when it wasn't actually happening."

Luke glances at me. "Isn't this the company that got Bailey…" He trails off.

"It is."

"Okay."

"We're looking for who set her up."

He blows out a long gust of air. "Okay, so you think it's someone in IT?"

"Or accounting. But you guys should be able to see who got into requisitions, right? Isn't there a log?"

"Yeah, but it's going to be a mess. I'll have to sift through everyone who got in the system."

"How long will it take to come up with a culprit?"

"Definitively? Many hours. A good guess? An hour or two."

"Let's go with the good guess to see if it matches who we think."

"Do I get to know that?" Luke starts typing madly.

"I'm going to hold off and see what you come up with."

"Okay, boss. And if Hammond asks what I'm up to?"

"Tell him I'm being outrageous and asking for ridiculous data. Then send him to me if he gets nosy."

"Do you think…" He trails out. "Never mind. Don't answer that. I'll start looking."

"Check in with me before lunch."

"Will do."

I glance out over the other cubicles. Another member of IT, a young woman, is settling into her desk. "Everything looks good otherwise? We were gone three business days."

"All looks good. Everything is operational. No problems."

"Great. Thanks."

I head back to my floor. It's quiet still. Gloria is usually the first to arrive, then the rest of HR.

But when I'm at my desk, staring at my monitor, it hits me that there is one task I've been forgetting.

Uncle Sherman.

The things I have to tell him are stacking up.

The accusations by Viola about marketing.

Firing my assistant.

Being wrong about firing my assistant.

Doing unspeakable things with my former and once again current assistant.

And now the whole trail of treachery that might involve marketing, accounting and IT.

And over what?

An employee wanting to bang me?

I remember Viola's behavior in my cabin. She could say anything she wanted about what happened behind that closed door. If she's in a snare, and already happy to throw a former best friend under the bus, am I next?

This fiasco is so Rhett. Party Rhett. Dumb Rhett. The Rhett who gets drunk in public, takes the wrong girl home, and gets pilloried in text messages when he can't remember who she is.

Uncle Sherman chose wrong.

I am not the man for this job.

None of my siblings or cousins, not even wild Jason, would get themselves in this big of a pickle.

I have to call him.

I pull out my cell phone, then realize it's barely seven. Uncle Sherman is no doubt an early riser, but he's also retired, so I don't feel comfortable ringing him at this hour.

Eight would be better.

A knock on the frame of the open door startles me.

Bailey stands there, delectable in my favorite office outfit of hers, a black jumpsuit that I can already imagine peeling down her body.

And in her hand?

The pink lip gloss.

Fuck.

I scoot up to the desk so she won't notice I'm already at full mast within ten seconds of looking at her.

"You okay, Rhett?" She heads for my desk, and I'm not sure where to look. Her breasts, slightly swaying beneath the soft fabric, as if her bra is lightweight or maybe, God, she doesn't have one on at all.

Yeah, I'm done for.

This is why bosses don't date anyone at the office. I'm not going to get a damn thing done.

"Please say you're wearing underwear." My words stumble over each other.

She glances back at the open door, then unfastens three of the satin buttons to reveal both glorious pink nipples. "Sorry. My sunburn makes it hard to wear my usual undergarments. Is that going to be a problem?"

Fuck. "Close the door."

"You sure?"

"Close the damn door."

She does as I tell her, but by the time she's got it latched, I have the pantsuit down to her waist.

I close in behind her, both hands on her bare breasts. "I'm never going to get a thing done with you around."

"Good." She wiggles her hips, and the suit falls to the floor. She steps out, naked other than a pair of ankle-breaking stilettos. "I couldn't wear shoes like this on the beach."

I can do nothing but look at her for a full minute, her skin glowing in the overhead light, shoulders tipped in pink, the skin that was beneath her bikini paler than the rest even though the strict tan lines are gone.

I sweep her into my arms and carry her to the sofa in the corner opposite the work desk, which is scattered with papers.

"The rest of the staff will be here any minute," I tell her.

"Then you better get on with it." She sits against the back of the sofa, her arms resting along the cushions. She spreads her knees wide, and fuck. I'm a goner. She still holds the lip gloss in her hand.

"I have one request," I say as I unbuckle my belt.

"You want to have sex with me while I put on my lip gloss?" She uncaps the top.

I pause. "How…"

"I thought about it later. I caught you watching me a

time or two, and I thought you might be thinking I was juvenile, wearing drugstore lip gloss."

"No, I spent way too much time thinking about it."

"I realized that somewhere on day two on the island." She looks down at my drooping pants. "So here you go." She spreads the silky gloss on her mouth.

And there's no stopping me. I'm on her, kissing the lip gloss right off her mouth. And I'm in her, enjoying the loud gasp that she makes.

Then she's laughing, hanging onto me, and we're moving together, making the sofa leather squeak.

I feel high, like I've won the lottery or climbed Everest. Her arms cling to my neck and we hold each other's gaze until her muscles tighten around me.

Her head falls back, and I unleash in her, her spasms releasing my own.

For a moment, we stay there, in that high, exultant place.

Then she squeals that we're making a mess on the sofa. And I watch her slide away, naked in those incredible shoes, bending over to snatch a handful of Kleenex, laughing as she cleans up the leather.

I want her again. I want my face in her. I want her in every direction.

Working with her will be impossible, but also the best.

I'll have to figure this out as I go.

35

BAILEY

I spend most of the morning getting my desk set up again, and experiencing extraordinary stickiness from the early encounter with Rhett. Thankfully, I packed a pair of panties in my purse.

And just before lunch, I get an unexpected visitor at my desk.

Kenna.

She's in an olive-green shirt dress that would be sassy with a belt, but I don't think Kenna believes in styling. She's an off-the-rack sort of girl.

"Hey," I say.

There is literally no reason Kenna could have for visiting me. We rarely encountered each other in my previous two years. She's an accounting clerk, not lowly enough to be a runner to Rhett's office, and not high up enough to consult with him on budget.

If she's here, it's way more likely she's doing a snoop job for Viola. I know all about those.

She must read my expression. "Viola's not in the office, and she hasn't answered any of my texts."

"Really?" She must have been tipped off. "Did she know I was coming back?"

"I think everyone knew after the dinner the final night on the cruise." Kenna perches on the corner of my desk, easy to do since it's mostly empty.

"How did she react?" I had been too into Rhett to notice her.

"Absolutely seething with a side of panic."

"Not surprising." I'm sure she knew if Rhett talked to me, we'd figure out what she did. I don't say that aloud, and I decide to keep my suspicion that she had help under my hat.

Kenna is in accounting. She could have been the helper. Maybe she's here to find out what I know about *her*.

Dang, corporate America can be tricky.

"Have you figured out what happened with marketing?" Kenna examines a pencil on my desk as if the answer doesn't interest her all that much, but my alarm bells start clanging.

I madly start typing and peer at my screen. "I don't care anymore. I'm trying to pick up where I left off."

"So you're rehired."

Did she think I was just here to bang the boss? I swallow a snotty response. "Yeah. The island time reminded us how well we work as a team."

Viola would have been completely snarky about that, but Kenna pokes at the eraser on the end of the pencil, not meeting my gaze.

She's acting awfully guilty.

"Well, if you hear anything about Viola, let me know. It would be hard for her to bail on her job. She has a lifestyle to keep, and she's always on the verge of maxing out her credit cards. She can't afford to quit without somewhere to go."

"You going to talk to HR?" Their offices are right across the hall.

"Nah. I'll see how it plays out." She hops off the desk and disappears into the corridor.

Now that was something. Kenna seemed cool and interesting on the cruise, but I'm not sure I can figure her out at all.

I order curry takeout for Rhett to eat with me in his office, and bring it in between his phone calls.

"Any word from Luke?" I ask, balancing both containers as I kick the door closed.

Rhett looks all business behind his desk in a white button-down, his suit jacket slung over the back of his tall leather chair.

"Yeah. He says it was definitely IT, and they knew what they were doing. The logs from eighteen days ago are deleted and unrecoverable."

So probably not Kenna. "They covered their tracks." I set his lunch in front of him.

He picks up the chopsticks. "Yup."

I sit opposite him and pop open my container. "Are we ever going to know who actually changed the requisitions?"

"Maybe not, but we do have the paper filings. Gloria

has pulled most of them." He slides a folder across the table.

I take a quick bite of curry, and I open to the first page. Each requisition to the fake company is on top of a paid requisition to the original company for the same amount, same date. Only the client ID, company name, and address have been changed. I flip through them. A few have additional notes about what was provided—the unnecessary logo, some old lead lists.

I aim the chopsticks at the pages. "So that proves I didn't even lose the company any money, although I brought you fake documents to sign."

Rhett tucks his tie inside his shirt to avoid getting food on it. I always loved watching him do that.

"And I signed them. I call that equally guilty."

"So what do we do?"

"Sarah insists on a company meeting."

I sit up straight. He's been talking to her about this? "What does she know?"

"She knew about the marketing issue from the beginning." He hesitates. "From before I fired you."

The curry becomes a lump in my belly. "Was she the one who told you to act quickly?"

"Sarah comes from a more cutthroat environment than Dougherty. It's her instinct to remedy a situation with swift, decisive action."

My face feels like it's on fire. "Then maybe she's not a good fit here."

Rhett maintains that controlled expression I associate with him before the cruise. "Sarah has been helpful to me. She has more experience."

I concentrate on slowing my breathing. Sarah can bite me. She's the reason Rhett didn't slow down and investigate before kicking me out of here.

Rhett lets out a long breath and leans over to cover my hand with his. He's back to being *my* Rhett. "Don't be upset, Bailey. It wasn't personal."

"It was to me."

"We're past it. Right? Now we're coming up with a solution."

"So fire Viola and keep an eye on IT. Back to business." I pull my hand away.

He sits back in his chair. "We don't have a solid case against her. She brought the problem to me, but I'm not sure she caused it, even though we know there are some circumstances that would point to her."

I leap from my chair. "You believed me on the island! We figured out a timeline, why she might have wanted me out of the way. You said she even came to your room!"

Rhett stands with me. "Bailey, I believe you. But none of that is actionable. I can't fire her over any of that. I need to show that she did more than bring me the problem. Without the logs, I can't do that."

"You were happy to fire *me* without logs."

He sits back down. "I was. I did. You're right."

I sit down, too. "There was more to it. You know that. I know it now. And I'm saying there is more to this than requisitions. It's personal."

Rhett presses his thumbs into his forehead. "I know."

"Have you told Dougherty yet? Is this something you

have to report? There's not any money lost, so maybe you don't."

"I haven't. And thank you for pointing that out. Without a budget issue, maybe it's simply an HR matter."

"Okay." The phone buzzes. I need to get it. I head for the door. "Viola isn't here today. If she's still gone tomorrow, I'll let HR know they have an issue to handle. They can deal with it. Maybe this will solve itself."

"That would be nice."

But as I head back to my desk, I wonder what other unsavory dealings might be going on at Dougherty. Trouble in IT. Sarah. Mysterious Dougherty himself.

There's a lot we don't know.

36

RHETT

On Wednesday morning, I leave yet another message for Uncle Sherman. He hasn't responded to anything I sent him yesterday.

I'm not even sure what to say at this point. Someone tried to fool me into firing my assistant? Maybe a woman who wants my attention?

This sounds ridiculous, and I'm glad he hasn't been available.

Sarah stops by my office in late morning and sits in the chair on the opposite side of my desk. It's unusual for her to come here unscheduled.

"What's going on?" I ask, rapidly finishing out the line I was typing.

"There's too much unrest for my liking."

I spin away from my monitor. "What do you mean?"

She sits tall in the chair, stiff in a dark green suit. "Hammond found Luke going through old logs and demanded to know what he was doing. Was that you?"

"Hammond went to you with it?"

Sarah sips from a coffee mug that reads, "If this is full, you're in danger."

Only after a pause long enough to raise my annoyance does she finally say, "Hammond stopped by your office. Which was locked. And you seemed…occupied." Her gaze briefly slides to the door, where Bailey sits outside.

My neck flares with heat. It's happening. Everything I thought would go down. And the thing is, I haven't laid a hand on Bailey today. Or yesterday afternoon. He must have come during my conference call with a client.

My reputation is shot. One damn cruise.

Now I'm a cliche. Boss and assistant.

And I drank too much on the beach. Party Rhett.

Sarah knows this about me. She was there.

But she's not being held accountable. She's not banging an employee.

She's not in charge.

Possibly abusing power.

Damn it.

Sarah takes another sip. "I urge you to call a company meeting this afternoon. Everyone other than the interns and part-timers. Be the boss. Be stern. Be your old self. We're on the rocks, Rhett. Steer us out of them." She stands to leave.

I have nothing to say.

When she's gone, I stare blankly at the monitor for long minutes.

I have to get myself back in order. Boss Rhett. Stern Rhett. Capable Rhett.

Bailey pops her head around the half-open door. "Everything okay?"

Maybe I've been too glib with Bailey. Maybe it's time to keep my cards closer to my chest.

I don't bother to soften my voice. "Call an all-hands meeting for two p.m."

Bailey frowns. "What should I say is the agenda?"

"Just a town hall. I'll come up with the agenda before two."

She slides into the chair Sarah occupied, her colorful skirt soft and flowing compared to Sarah's stiff suit. "What did she say? You know I'm not fond of her."

Another reason to separate these elements of my job. "I need to right the ship. I'll figure out what to say. Did Viola come back?"

"No."

"Okay, that's one thing, at least."

"Are you going to mention her?"

"Unlikely."

"Are you going to mention me?"

"Only that you have been restored to your position following a more thorough look at the situation."

She sits very still, her gaze on her hands. "Was this the wrong move?"

"What?"

"Bringing me back?"

Everything I'm trying to keep stern and tough begins to soften. She's my kryptonite. "Gloria was highly complimentary of your organization when she took over. I'll be using her as a basis of the reasoning for your reinstatement."

Although I'm sure people like Hammond will have other ideas. Sarah, too, obviously.

A rap on the door makes us both turn.

It's Gloria. "Oh! Bailey's here. I can come back."

Bailey stands. "I'm all done. Rhett, I'll get that memo out." She turns to Gloria. "We're having a company meeting at two."

"Oh!" Gloria says. She glances between us.

Even though she was quite properly on the opposite side of my desk, and we were discussing work, my neck still feels on fire. It's like Gloria is also wondering what we were up to. I'm not going to be able to shake this.

When Bailey is gone, Gloria sets a folder on my desk. "I wasn't going to bother you with this, but since Viola seems to have disappeared, and the investigation into her marketing requisitions is ongoing, I thought you might want to see it."

I pull the folder forward and open the front cover.

It's Viola's HR folder. It begins with her original application, her government forms, and several performance reviews, which seem adequate.

"Turn one more page," Gloria says.

The next file is an HR complaint against Viola by Toby Barnsdale from the IT department. It was six months ago. Viola repeatedly insisted Toby work on her computer station, refusing any other member of the department. Toby was uncomfortable around her because they had formerly dated.

"She's broken the fraternization rule multiple times, but I'm not sure how enforceable it is between departments anyway," Gloria says. "We're mainly watching for power dynamics." She stops talking abruptly, and I know she's just realized I'm seeing my assistant. The ultimate power imbalance.

I can't do anything about that. I'm not firing Bailey, and I'm not giving her up either. "We're going to strike that anyway. Today might be a good time."

"At your company meeting?" Gloria asks.

I don't think she intends for it to sound as snarky as it comes across.

"Probably not quite yet," I say.

"There's more," she says.

The next page is a complaint by an intern who used to work in marketing. She says that Viola stalked her after seeing her talk to Toby Barnsdale. She felt uncomfortable. She left the company three months ago.

"I added a printout in there from another HR folder since it seemed to apply here," Gloria says.

I flip the page. This one is a performance review for Blake Samuels in IT, dated a month ago. He got low marks for incomplete tasks, time away from his desk, and altering files not in his scope of work. Hammond conducted it.

I sit forward. "What files did he alter?"

"We'll have to see if Hammond knows. I asked around, and it seems Blake was spending an inordinate amount of time near Viola's desk."

"Is he here today?"

"That's the kicker. Nobody's seen him since the cruise."

But Viola came to my room. Surely she wouldn't have done that if she was seeing this Blake fellow.

Unless she's simply manipulating him to do her bidding.

I stare at Blake's performance form. There's no picture. Was this the guy she was sitting with at the pool when I got back to the ship?

We could have our culprit. I need to visit Hammond.

"I appreciate this," I tell Gloria. "Can I hang onto this file?"

"Sure. I'll snag it if I need to close it out."

"And she hasn't even called in?"

"Nope. Blake neither. It's like they both vanished."

Huh. "Well, thank you."

When she's gone, I buzz Hammond, but he doesn't answer.

The meeting memo dings on my computer. Bailey's sent it out.

I work straight through lunch. Bailey brings me a sandwich from my favorite shop, but we don't exchange any random talk.

It's better this way. Keep our personal matters to after hours.

At two o'clock, I pick up my card with a few scrawled notes. I need to address Bailey's return to our office. Make a few jokes about the cruise. And focus on projections and quarterly reports. Get us past the rumors and back to business.

I'll grab Hammond afterward to talk about Blake Samuels.

It's a good plan.

When I step inside the large meeting room lined with rows of chairs, the majority of the company is assembled. Bailey sits in the front row, pen poised over a notebook.

"Hello, everyone. I assume you've all recovered from the excitement of the cruise? I think I've had enough beach to last me a good long time."

There's muted laughter. Good start.

"Our head of human resources, Gloria Rivers, was good enough to bring me binders of paperwork during the trip—see, it wasn't all play and no work."

I pause for their low laughs.

"And between that data and some conversations with my assistant Bailey Johansson, we realized we acted too hastily on some matters involving requisitions that had been incorrectly categorized."

I spot Sarah nodding in approval.

All right. This is good.

There are no snarky remarks, not that I expected any to my face, but nobody seems to be whispering either.

I keep going. "So effective yesterday, Bailey has resumed her position with my apologies for not digging deeply enough before that hasty action."

Eyes shift in her direction. She gives a small wave then swiftly starts writing on her paper like her life depends on it.

Rather than allow time for any questions that I might not be ready to field, I plow forward. "Now, let's focus on the third-quarter projections."

I'm about to launch into it when the door to the room flies open so hard that the handle smacks the wall with a loud crack.

Everyone turns to the sound.
Great.
It's Viola.

37

BAILEY

Holy hotcakes, Viola just crashed the company meeting.

She's not dressed for work, wearing denim shorts and a red tank top. Her hair is in a messy top knot.

For a moment, I'm not sure what to do. I look up at Rhett, who is perfectly composed in his gray pinstripe suit.

Gloria stands. "Viola, let's head to my office to discuss your absences."

"I don't think so," Viola says. "I know what he's up to. I know why he called this meeting." Her face is an angry snarl, all slanted brows and red lipstick.

"Viola," Rhett says, "I think Gloria is right. There might be a conversation you need to have in private first."

But Viola continues to make her way along the wall to the front. Her eyes are wild, like she has nothing to lose. I have to admit, I'm feeling a little shaky and clutch my notebook to my chest.

"I get the company emails on my phone. I saw this meeting get called. It might have been from your account but I recognize when Bailey sends it. You two are plotting." She points a finger at Rhett. "You probably think you can talk trash about me in front of the whole staff, but I'm here to talk about *you*!"

What does she mean by that? Is she going to give Rhett grief for dating me when she was trying to get him herself?

"Viola, this is not the time nor the place—" Rhett says, but Viola cuts him off.

"Oh, this is a great time. You've been planning to fire me, haven't you? Just like with Bailey before you started banging her. Shoot first and ask questions later! But I didn't have anything to do with those messed up requisitions! I brought them to you because I knew there was a problem! And my boss was it!"

The room breaks out in murmurs. I turn to Marney, the head of marketing, who is sitting on my row. Her feet are crossed in her orthopedics, and she shakes her head like Viola is a naughty child about to get a time-out.

Rhett holds his composure. "Why don't you tell Gloria all about it in her office?"

"No!" Viola says. "I know you don't like me or want me. I got the message on the cruise. You got want you wanted." She gestures to me, spawning a new wave of chatter in the room. "But I will not let you two pin this on me!"

Gloria steps forward to take Viola by the arm.

"Viola, this is enough. Come with me, so I don't have to call security."

But Viola shakes her off. "I know about you, Rhett Armstrong. I figured it out. I know all about you."

She shakes off Gloria and slinks up to Rhett.

I expect Rhett to be bemused and confident, maybe a little condescending.

But a trickle of sweat slides from his forehead to his ear.

What does Viola have on him?

I feel sick. Did he have some secret affair with her that I don't know about?

Do I know him at all?

Did I know *her* at all?

But her next words bring out the real reason for her visit.

She stabs his chest. "You're a fake. A charity hire. Your big ol' Uncle Sherman Packwood Pickle had to bail out your worthless self by starting a company and giving it to you because you weren't ever going to amount to a damn thing on your own." She pokes him again. "You aren't qualified to do jack shit here, and now everybody knows it. Nobody calls a man they believe in 'Mr. Juicy.'"

Murmurs break out.

I can barely catch my breath. Rhett's uncle started this company just for Rhett? He's the secret Dougherty?

I suddenly remember our conversation on the boat right before the formal dinner. I'd told him how awful the world was when only the connected could get anywhere.

Rhett was exactly that!

Oh, God!

I switch to watching Rhett, who can't seem to pull himself together. He obviously didn't want anyone to know about his uncle.

But Viola isn't through. She catches my eye for a minute, then turns back to Rhett. "And we all know you like hiring people you want a *piece* of."

Okay, that's it. Viola is going *down*.

I drop my notebook to the floor and race forward. I grab Viola by both arms and jerk them behind her back. Only when I've dragged her to the door do I realize everyone is seated in dumb silence.

I vaguely hear Sarah ask, "Is that true, Rhett?" before I get Viola in the hall.

"What the hell are you doing?" I ask her. "You know what you did."

She whirls hard and breaks her arms free. "I know no such thing, Bailey, you treacherous bitch. I asked him not to fire you. I told him it wasn't your fault. Now get off me. I'm out of here, anyway."

She stalks down the hall. I follow her to the elevator. "So you're quitting?"

She stabs the button, then thinks better of it and heads farther down for the stairwell. "This place is a disaster waiting to happen."

She takes off down the stairs. I wait at the door, pondering what she said. Did she stick up for me? If so, why the silence after?

I don't believe her.

But I have to get back to Rhett. He's bound to be reeling after all this.

The hallway fills with employees leaving the meeting, most of them skipping the elevator in favor of the stairs.

Gloria pushes through them to get to me, almost tripping on her long blue maxi dress. "Come with me, Bailey. We need to craft a carefully worded message to go out to the staff."

I look behind her to see if I can spot Rhett, but there is no getting past the sea of employees, all chattering with alarm.

"I need to find Rhett," I tell her. It's imperative that he knows I'm with him, even if I did go off about exactly the same situation as his arrangement with his uncle only a few days ago. God, he's going to think I resent him now.

I have to fix it.

"I already tried," Gloria says. "Come with me."

I don't want to go with her, but she leads me past the HR cubicles to her office and closes the door. "We have to spin this quickly. The department heads are already calling a meeting."

Now she has my attention. "Why?"

She sits down. "There's too much that's happened too fast, the marketing snafu, you getting fired, you showing up, you two seeming…together. The news that Dougherty isn't what we thought comes at a bad time. They have concerns about the company."

I drop into a chair in the corner. "I should talk to Rhett about this."

"He's not available."

That again. "What do you mean, he's not available? He was leading the meeting."

"He left by the back door. That leads straight to his office."

"Then I'm sure he's at his desk. Let me talk to him." I stand up.

"He's not. I checked."

"What do you mean? Did you text him? Call him?"

"Both. He's not answering."

This isn't like Rhett at all. I sit back down. "Where did he go?"

Gloria pinches her lips like she's trying to calm herself. "If I knew, I wouldn't have you in here. So let's do this. We need damage control."

"Let me text him."

"You can try, but we also need to craft this message."

I can't do that. Not yet. "Meet me in his office in three minutes." I jump up and lunge for the door. I have to see this for myself.

The staff has returned to their desks, other than a few HR employees talking near their cubicles. They glance up at me, but I blow past them.

My desk is empty. Rhett's door is open.

I glance inside. He's not there.

To be sure, I check his private bathroom. Nope.

I go into the short hallway that leads to the second door of the main meeting room.

I poke my head into the now-empty room, the rows of chairs slightly askew from the abrupt ending.

No one.

He must have gone down the elevator while I was at the other end of the hall with Viola at the stairwell.

I return to my desk and pull out my cell phone. No texts.

I send him a quick message.

Hey. Are you okay? Nobody cares about your uncle. Talk to me.

I'm still staring at it, hoping for a response, when Gloria shows up.

"He'll write me. I know it," I tell her.

"I'm sure he will. But until then, let's handle it."

I turn to my computer. "The message to the staff?"

"Yes. I don't know where he's taken off to, but having three staff members MIA is not going to help the situation. Let's send a message, an official one from his office, and calm this down."

I want to jump in my car, find Rhett. Go to his house, maybe.

But I know she's right. We should handle this. He's obviously not going to.

So we do. We craft a message about Viola's outburst, that we will look into everything, and to proceed with the day's work.

But Rhett doesn't message me.

Not that day.

Not that night.

And the next morning, he doesn't come in.

I sit at his desk, looking out the window, wondering what the heck is going on. So what if he was a given the company by family?

But that niggling feeling that I hadn't helped matters really digs in.

This is a lot.

Three missing employees, including the CEO.

Huge accusations.

An improper relationship.

Could all this actually bring down a company?

I sense someone entering the room and spin around.

It's not Rhett, but I see the resemblance.

Broad-shouldered, mid-sixties, handsome, and looking exactly like the man Viola and I saw so many times in those karaoke videos of Rhett and his family.

Sherman Packwood Pickle.

38

RHETT

This is more like it.

Axel and I look over the mountainside, the evergreens curving down the hill in an alignment so perfect that you know Mother Nature had a master plan when she created Colorado.

Havannah's castle sits in the distance, flags flying from the upper turrets. I make out a few tiny cars in the parking lot surrounding it.

"She regrets not building a garage from the beginning," Axel says. "I think she's going to tear out the surface lots with the next renovation."

I shield my eyes from the glare. "The asphalt does hurt the illusion that you've slipped into another era."

"That's what she said." Axel turns to look up at the summit. "Mom is expecting us for lunch." He heads back down the path.

I don't respond to that, glad for the gorgeous day anywhere that isn't Miami.

And out in nature, not an office building. And with my youngest brother, not the disenchanted employees of Dougherty Inc.

Uncle Sherman buzzed me this morning. It was five a.m. here but a more reasonable seven on the East Coast.

I didn't answer. He's just returning my calls from the previous days. It can wait.

Everything can wait.

That terrible meeting.

Viola, exposing the secret in front of the entire staff.

The uproar.

The horror.

Bailey, whose big disappointment in life is not having the connections she needed to reach her dream, now working for someone whose entire career was built by nepotism.

All behind me.

For now, it's me, the mountain, and Axel.

Hopefully up here, things will become clear.

We make it down in time to quickly shower and drive over to my parents' house, which is one parcel over from Axel's. Mom kisses our heads and serves us our favorite black beans and brisket over rice.

Eating it settles me, like I've done the right thing. Gone home to figure things out.

Mom looks the same, although she's assimilated to Colorado in how she dresses with jeans, a fitted T-shirt, and hiking shoes. Her hair is twisted up, partially held back by sunglasses.

"This is such a nice surprise," she says, sitting down opposite us. "Rhett, I didn't know you were coming for a visit."

I have no easy way of explaining why I came, so I smile and take another bite of rice.

She serves a helping onto her plate. "Axel says you got in late last night. How long are you staying?"

I swallow. "Not sure."

Axel swirls his tea glass. "He bought a one-way ticket."

Mom sets her fork down. "Is something wrong at the office?"

Now I can't eat another bite. It's one thing to disappoint Uncle Sherman. But by coming here, I've involved Mom.

"He's not ready to talk about it," Axel says. "We'll weasel it out of him soon."

Mom's gaze remains on my face, as if she can read my mind through my expression. I force myself to shovel another mouthful of brisket into my mouth.

She lets us eat quietly for a while, but I can see the wheels turning as she watches both of us.

"Rhett is staying at your house, I take it?"

"Yup." Axel sets his napkin on the table. "We're heading over to the castle to help fix the fence for the donkeys after this. They haven't been able to roam with the outer gate down."

"That's nice. Havannah doesn't have enough help?"

"Oh, she does, but we like doing it. It's good to talk to her."

"Say hello to Calypso."

Axel stands. "Will do. We best get going."

"Thanks for lunch, Mom," I say.

We both pick up our plates and take them to the kitchen.

"She's onto you," Axel whispers as we scrape our leftovers into the compost bin.

"Well, keep her off me."

We hush when Mom follows us in with the platter. "Will I see you boys for dinner soon?"

"For sure. We'll text you." Axel kisses her cheek. I do the same, and then we're off. Out the door and into his SUV, bouncing down the gravel road to get to the castle.

"Speaking of women," Axel says, "someone keeps looking at their phone whenever the name Bailey comes up. Who's that and why aren't you responding?"

I don't know what to tell Axel about the mess I'm in. So far, we've only made small talk about hiking and meeting Mom. Nothing serious.

"She's my assistant at Dougherty."

He focuses on the road a while before saying, "Seems like you'd have no problem answering if she's an assistant."

My family is too perceptive for their own good.

"How are things with Calypso?"

"No redirects. I'm not the one who showed up halfway across the country in the middle of the night. Either you killed somebody or you're running from a woman."

"Let's go with murder."

"I don't think you have it in you, bro."

I stare out the window as majestic fir trees whiz by. "It's everything," I finally say. The story feels too big. The requisitions. The firing. The cruise. The rescue. It's laughable, like a movie plot, not real life. So I simply tell him, "Someone found out Uncle Sherman was the owner of Dougherty."

Axel glances over at me, his hands tapping the steering wheel. "That shouldn't matter, right? The company is doing well."

I don't know how to explain it to him. He wrote his own app and sold it for a ton of money. He's never worked for anyone or felt responsible for the livelihood of an entire staff.

I blow out a gust of air. "It should never have been a secret. Secrets tend to make waves when they're found out."

"That's definitely a thing. So did they run you out or did you run yourself out?"

"I just left. They're all capable. It will be fine for a while."

We turn onto the castle grounds, the sprawling towers in front of us jutting into the sky. "And what happens when it's not actually fine?"

"I don't know." And I really don't. I can't face all that at the moment. Bailey, mainly. I'm exactly what she said. A product of connections. Choking out the real talent. Viola was right, too. Everything going wrong at the company falls squarely on me.

We drive around the castle on the service road and pull up next to the barn in the back. Ever since our cousin Sunny married the Prince of Avalonia, the whole Pickle clan has had an obsession with Avalonia's miniature laughing donkeys, a special breed only found there. Avalonia's mountain regions are similar in terrain and climate to Colorado, so Havannah brought a small herd to her castle as an extra experience for her guests.

The moment we exit the SUV, I can hear their soft *hee haw* bray that dissolves into *ha ha ha*.

Axel pulls a toolbox from the back seat. "I'd say you're lucky to be getting so much outdoors and sunshine after being an office rat, but you look healthy and tan."

"We just had a company cruise," I tell him.

"Oh, right, on Blue Sapphire. I'll have to book one of those sometime."

"They're good." I don't add, 'unless you're stranded on their private island and they don't do a headcount.' I don't want to get into any of that.

We head for the barn. The donkeys are mostly in the feeding pen, braying longingly at the larger outer sections of the grounds.

Axel hops over the wood fence. "Don't worry, little donkeys. We'll get you back to your stomping grounds."

I try not to feel self-conscious as the donkeys mill around me, all laughing with their signature *hee haw ha ha ha*. Axel is a good distance away, about to hop the second fence, so I tell them, "Don't you know it's not nice to kick a man when he's down?"

They keep laughing, weaving in and around me as I catch up to Axel.

We arrive at the damaged section of the fence. A

minor avalanche of rocks and uprooted trees have fallen on it, taking out several yards.

Havannah herself is out there, her hand on her back to balance her enlarged belly. She's expecting her second baby in a few months.

She tells a crew of four men where to place the trees after they're cut up and turns to us. "Oh, good. More help. Rhett! So good to see you. It was the Haunted Ball last, right?"

I step in for a quick hug. "It was. Looks like you've been busy."

She pats her striped belly. "I have. I'm worried about more trees falling when the herd is out, so we're going to pull down this section of fence and expand over there." She points to the right, farther from the base of the hill. "It will be safer for them."

"So we should start pulling down this section of fence?" Axel asks.

"Yes. Save what lumber you can. We'll reuse it over there. The rest of the crew is moving the rocks and cutting up the trees."

It's steady work that requires little concentration. We unbolt the heavy sections of the fence and carry the wood to its new location. Havannah goes inside, and we work through the afternoon. I feel the occasional buzz of a message in my pocket, but it's easy to ignore. There's always another bolt, another section of fence.

When the crew calls it a day, we also stop.

Axel mops his forehead with a bandanna, watching as I glance at my phone and tuck it back in my pocket.

"You know, you can't hide here forever," he says.

"You kicking me out after all this work?"

He smacks my back. "Of course not. But I'm just saying. The piper will come to be paid."

I know he's right, but I'm not ready to face any of it.

39

BAILEY

I jump from Rhett's chair, feeling guilty for getting caught sitting there. What must it look like to Sherman that I'm in Rhett's seat?

My entire face flames. "Hello."

Sherman waves me to sit down. "You look good in that chair. You must be Rhett's right-hand woman. Bailey, is it?"

I wonder if he ever knew I was fired. It doesn't seem like it.

"And you must be Uncle Sherman."

"I've been outed it seems. The young lady at reception could barely get a word out. I sure would like to meet the whippersnapper who figured it out. I was trying to be the strong, silent type, at least on this one. It's not normally my style."

I picture him with his sons and extended family, belting out "Fight for Your Right to Party" like the Gen-X rebel he likely is.

"I bet not," I say, although I'm not sure how to

address his request. Viola is as impossible to find as Rhett at the moment. And the rogue IT guy.

Things are a bit of a mess at the moment.

"Rhett didn't come in today, at least not so far," I tell him.

"That's what I understand from the front desk. He's been trying to get in touch with me for a few days. I flew to the Atlanta airport to pursue the possibility of a Pickle franchise in Terminal A, and decided to make a stop here on the way back."

I'm not sure how much to tell him. "We had a meeting yesterday where your role in the creation of Dougherty was revealed. I take it you wanted Rhett to keep it a secret."

"I did. It can be a real trial proving yourself when you're saddled with nepotism. It becomes the de facto reason why you fail, even though failure is the fastest track to success."

"You think so?"

He leans forward, bracing his elbows on the opposite side of Rhett's desk. "I know so. If I hadn't played it so safe in my early years, I might have had fifty Pickle delis, not five. So I'm encouraging all the kids to take big chances."

"Dougherty is doing well."

"I've seen that. I had a feeling strategy and analysis would be a good fit for Rhett. He's a natural at spotting a problem and being unrelenting about finding a way to fix it."

"But management is a different skill." Only after I say it do I realize that I might not ought to question

Sherman. Dougherty is at a pivotal moment with its CEO MIA.

But he laughs. "On that score, you are totally right. This company grew faster than the experience level of my nephew. So here we are." He glances around. "So what made him take off, exactly?"

I describe the issue with marketing and how there was a conflict with some staff and possibly some IT involvement in changing records. I leave out the interpersonal stuff with Viola and Rhett and myself.

"I think the reveal of your role in making Rhett the head of the company may have come at exactly the wrong moment," I tell him.

"And so my nephew has retreated." Sherman sits back in his chair, the fingers on both hands pressed together. "He hasn't answered my calls today. Yours?"

I shake my head. "Our head of HR has been trying, too."

"Is this out of character for him?"

"It is. I've been his assistant for two years, and he's always been so intense. I can't imagine what would make him simply…leave."

"Did anything else happen? Not that there needs to be more. Did you all just come back from the cruise?"

Oh. That. "Well, there were some irregularities there."

"Were there? Did the atmosphere get too casual? Rhett is quite the reveler."

"He is?"

Sherman chuckles, and it's so like Rhett's that my heart skitters. "I've been blessed with a great variety of temperaments among the younger generations of the Pickle family. Rhett is like my oldest, Jason. Wild. Charismatic. Possibly not the most dedicated to work."

This is weird. "I hate to contradict you, but Rhett has been the most demanding, diligent, unrelenting member of this company since the get-go."

"He's got a chip on his shoulder. That might be my doing." Sherman falls silent, tapping his fingers together. "We're going to have to fix this. But what were these irregularities?"

Back to that. "There was a storm. Quite a few staff members got sick."

"No one seriously?"

"No." I hesitate. "And during the evacuation, Rhett was left behind on the private island when the ship left."

Sherman's hands fall to the armrests with a thump. "Alone? During a tropical storm?"

And here it is. "Not totally alone. I was there, too."

Sherman relaxes against the backrest. "I see."

I'm not going to say another dang thing.

We're quiet a moment, the faint buzz of a copier from HR the only sound making it through the open office door.

"And you're okay? You're both okay?"

I fiddle with the pens on Rhett's desk. "We're fine."

"How long were you alone?"

"Two nights."

"Oh." Now he's looking at me differently, and I feel like he can absolutely imagine what we were up to.

"We were fine," I add.

"Did you have food?"

"There was a bucket of pickles."

This gets a great guffaw from Sherman. "Of course."

This will be okay. Sherman isn't going to judge us. "We made Pickle margaritas. There were mix packets. We were fine."

"Pickles and margaritas. I bet that was a fine time while you waited for the boat to come back." He watches me closely as he asks his next question. "So, what do you think has happened to Rhett?"

"I don't think he panicked, because I don't think he has it in him." I clasp my hands tightly together to stop fidgeting. "But he's spooked. And if he won't answer us, I don't know how to unspook him."

"I think you're right. Several of the boys are intensely self-reflective. His brother Axel is, too. And my Anthony."

"Do you have any ideas where he would go?"

"Has anyone gone to his house?"

"I don't think so."

Sherman stands. "Let's head that way. Meanwhile, I'll make some calls."

40

RHETT

Axel and I sit on our parents' back deck drinking beer to celebrate Friday even though only Dad had to work it.

Midsummer in Colorado is never as brutal as it can be in Florida. As hot as the days can get in the mountains, the nights are cool and breezy. It's not like Miami, where it feels like a sauna even after dark.

We're all in shorts and light flannel shirts, which seem to be the uniform for evening here. A huge sectional wicker sofa topped with thick cushions gives the four of us plenty of room to spread out.

My parents moved to Boulder after I graduated, although the two youngest, Axel and Nadia, finished school here. It's never been home to me, but I like it. The house and woods might be different from what I knew growing up, but the furniture is the same, and Mom cooks our favorites. It's good. It takes me back, like a visit with family will do.

I have no idea what I'm doing, really. I have to go

back sometimes, or else relinquish the company. And then what? Work my way up somewhere else? Reject the gift Uncle Sherman gave me?

It's a mess.

But here is good. Here is a reprieve.

We watch headlights make a meandering path through the trees. The deck overlooks the back and right side of the property, which is where the private drive from the highway approaches the house.

"You invite somebody else to the party?" Dad asks.

"Nope," Axel says, setting his beer on the pine coffee table.

Dad heaves his boots off the wicker ottoman and sets his beer down. "I'll see who it is."

I'm unconcerned until I see Mom's foot wiggling ninety to nothing. That's her tell that she's anxious about what she's done.

I listen. The woods are quiet and deep beyond the deck, and sound echoes easily off the mountainside. We hear the crunch of the car approaching, then the slam of the doors. Dad's deep voice greets them.

Soon, I figure out why Mom is so antsy. I recognize my uncle's voice.

"Mom?" I say.

"He called this morning," she said. "You haven't been answering your phone."

"And you told him I was here." I work hard to stuff down my annoyance. She isn't part of this. She wouldn't have lied about my whereabouts if her brother-in-law asked.

"Go talk to him," she says.

Axel's gaze is on me as I haul myself up from the sofa. It's like all the times I got busted staying out late and he and Nadia watched in silence while I got bawled out by Dad.

Mom reaches out to touch my arm. "And you all come back out here once you've settled things."

"Sure." I set my beer down with the others. Looks like the drinking is over for the moment.

But when I step inside the house, another voice stops me in my tracks.

"It's nice to meet you, Mr. Armstrong."

What is Bailey doing here?

I had assumed this was about my failure to follow up with Uncle Sherman.

But if she's here…

"There he is," Dad says, turning as I enter the expansive living room. "Alive and well."

Bailey seems small next to my uncle, who could make a linebacker look average. She gives a little wave.

"I always like a jaunt to the mountains," Sherman says. "I was traveling all week, anyway. "Good to see you, boy."

I shake his hand, my eyes shifting to take in him, then Bailey, then my dad.

"This looks like a business meeting," Dad says. "I'll be out on the deck. Plenty of beer for everyone when you're ready."

"Thank you, Mr. Armstrong," Bailey says.

"It's Ronan," Dad says. "No pretense here."

Bailey nods, but she seems nervous. Meeting the parents. And under these circumstances. I suppose there have been worse. Yeah, looking at Sherman's kids, all those situations were wild.

And this is about a lot more than Bailey.

I sit down on the sofa, and Sherman takes a chair nearby. Bailey chooses the loveseat opposite us.

Time to pay the piper, as Axel said.

Uncle Sherman takes the lead. "Rhett, when I established Dougherty for you five years ago, the only reason I wanted to be a silent partner was to make clear you were in charge. Maybe you did have an angel investor, and maybe he was in the family, but you were still at the helm. I took a hands-off approach and let you sink or swim. I never wanted you to carry the burden of having your employees believe you were anything but the perfect person for the company. Sometimes people can jump to conclusions when they see a relationship behind a choice of leadership. I wanted to spare you that."

I glance over at Bailey. She's sitting primly in a navy suit I remember from before I fired her. Her eyes meet mine, and she gives a small smile.

I'm not sure what she's here for. The company? Me? Everything about her is old Bailey, tirelessly professional, maybe a little exasperated.

I sit back on the cushions, trying to appear nonchalant even though I'm anything but. "I take it you went to Dougherty if Bailey is here."

"It was an easy stop on my travels. Didn't expect to see you had bailed."

I have no answer for that.

We're all quiet for a minute. I'm not sure what anyone is here for.

It's a game of chicken for a while, everyone waiting to see who will speak next.

Bailey breaks first. "We need you back there. Gloria and I sent out a company bulletin about the meeting. We explained that Dougherty was and always has been a family company and that it wasn't any secret. We downplayed Viola's big announcement."

Uncle Sherman nods along. "Sounds like it's well in hand."

"What about the marketing problem?"

Sherman turns to Bailey.

She speaks up. "The logs were deleted, but Hammond was able to cross reference the timing of the changes and the deletion with the late shift, which brought the number of suspects down to Georgia High and Blake Samuels."

I sit forward, "But Blake is——"

"Exactly. The missing IT guy who used to date Viola. Gloria told me about him."

"You think he was trying to get Viola in trouble?"

Bailey nods. "Yeah, and she passed the trouble right on to me."

"Viola insisted you weren't guilty," I say. "And she brought that up again at the meeting."

Bailey tucks her crossed ankles under the chair. She's the picture of prim and proper in front of Uncle Sherman. "I think she was so clueless about what was happening, she didn't realize that someone had done it to harm her and was trying to protect me. The memos were directed to Marney, probably as a way to get Viola fired. Marney must have passed them right on to Viola without looking at them."

Now I get it. "Which is why Viola said she was the only one doing any work."

Uncle Sherman grunts. "So I suppose you call in this Blake fellow, follow up with Marney and Viola, and then what?"

"Blake's still missing," Bailey says. "I'm guessing we won't see him again. I assumed that Viola was the one upset that you and I were discussing this and would figure it out, but apparently it was Blake."

"Viola was the target. You were collateral damage."

Bailey shrugs. "Sounds like it."

Uncle Sherman stands. "Well, it seems you all have it well in hand. Rhett, it's your company, you can fire who you like. But I'm betting Bailey's underutilized and probably should have a bigger role in your company than your assistant. That's all I will say on the matter." He turns to Bailey. "It's been lovely meeting you. I will be out on the next flight in the morning. I think I will have a drink with Ronan and Caprice while you two settle things out."

I stand to shake his hand. "Thank you for bringing her, Uncle Sherman."

"I wouldn't let go of a woman like that," he says. "Not if you know what's good for you."

Then he's through the back door, out of view.

Bailey waits on the love seat, her hands clasped together.

I'm not sure what to say.

"You left us," she says. "Not just the company. But

me. You didn't respond to texts. You didn't answer calls." She draws in a deep breath. "I deserve better than that."

Damn. She's right. "You do. There's no excuse."

"Nope."

Now that Uncle Sherman is gone, I can see she's upset. She's revealing it to me, bit by bit.

I walk to the loveseat, but instead of sitting next to her, I kneel before her. She allows me to take her hand, and relief washes over me. I was afraid she'd pull away.

"Do you remember when you talked about how frustrating it was to get passed over for people who were well connected, who had family and contacts who got them what they wanted?"

She nods. "I thought about that conversation a lot after you left."

"You were right. You're still right. It is frustrating that this is the way so much of the world works. So when everything was falling apart, and then I got called out in front of the whole company for that very thing, and you had just told me about your situation—the unfairness of all of it made me not want to do it anymore."

She shakes her head. "It's not your fault that your uncle wants this for you."

"But it is my fault if I disappoint everyone when given that opportunity. If I get to keep it because I'm his nephew."

"I don't think it's as bad as that, Rhett." She pokes my chest. "You have to be resilient. You can't be so rigid that if things go awry, you snap in two. You have to bend. You have to admit your mistakes. And you have to be up front about who you are."

"But what if I'm a slacker who'd rather coast than be in charge?"

"Don't limit your definition of yourself to who you used to be, Rhett. You're also a control freak who insists on perfection and absolute dominance in our field. Can't you find an in between?"

I hadn't so far. "I don't know."

"Then get a business coach. Someone who can help you figure out what you excel at, and a schedule that allows both work Rhett and play Rhett to have time. Someone who can help you figure out how to present yourself in front of your employees as both their leader and part of a larger family-based brand of companies. Lots of great corporations are built on family. Just stop pretending yours isn't."

"I can do that."

"None of this is all or nothing. It's not stay or quit. It's not fire someone or endure them. We can all learn and shift and adapt."

"You think Viola should stay?"

"I'm not sure about that, but we should probably listen to her."

"I hope you mean Gloria should listen to her. I'm never going to be alone in a room with her again after the bikini incident."

Bailey holds up a hand. "I don't think I want to know about that. And yes, let Gloria handle that. It's her job. You have people, Rhett. Good people. Let them do their work."

"What about my reputation as Mr. Juicy?"

"Rhett, it was a nickname put out by thirsty single women. And maybe a few married ones. Don't fret about it. There are others."

"Really? Like who?"

"Like Mike in accounting, the one who wears the tight pants."

"He does?"

"He's known as Foot Long. We're jerks, Rhett. Thirsty jerks. Don't worry about that."

"Okay. Forgotten. So I get coaching. Viola gets a second chance. Blake is obviously out, not that he's returning." I hesitate. "What about us?"

"I think you should get a different assistant," I tell him. "I don't think I can work so closely with you without us scandalizing the staff."

Her words melt into me. "Done. So we're okay?"

She smiles. "Of course we're okay. I didn't expect you to flip out on me, but geez, we've been together on a personal level for less than a week. I don't expect you to lean on me yet. Give it time."

"But we'll get that time." I kiss the back of her hand. "I want that time."

She wraps both of her hands around mine. "We'll get that time. But whatever is going to happen between me and you, we should have some separation between our roles at Dougherty. I'll help you hire a new assistant."

"And what will you do?"

"Since this is purely a nepotism role, I'd say go with Sherman's idea."

"Sure. VP? Of what department?"

"Currently we only have a VP of operations. I think marketing needs some leadership. Marney isn't cutting it."

"So VP of marketing?"

She nods. "Gotten purely based on me banging Mr. Juicy. Everyone will know exactly why I got promoted."

I laugh. "And you'll be so good at it, it won't matter."

"Exactly." She wraps her legs around my waist. "And eventually, I'll have the experience I need to move into the field I always wanted."

"This sounds like a plan." I slide my hands under her and pull her close. "And meanwhile, you better pleasure the boss so he'll keep you as his favorite."

She taps my nose. "Or maybe, he better pleasure me or I'll expose his incompetence."

I bite her finger. "I like this. I like it a lot."

She wraps her arms around my neck. "You better. Because I have plans for a new office that will need breaking in."

"Mmm. Order a big fluffy rug."

She nuzzles her nose against my cheek. "I like your workplace suggestions. Keep them coming."

Just before my mouth covers hers, I say, "I'll keep *you* coming."

41

BAILEY

One month later

I'm on my knees, adjusting the placement of a furry white area rug in front of a sleek red leather sofa, when Rhett appears in the doorway of my new office.

"I have those projections you asked for from accounting. Matthew delivered them an hour ago."

I stand up, checking the location of the rug. "And you waited a whole hour to get them to me?" I put my hands on my hips and look at him sternly. It's our favorite game. "Close the door so I can show you how displeased I am."

He closes the door and locks it. In seconds, we're on the rug, his body on top of mine. "I told you putting your office on the same floor as mine was a bad idea," he says against my neck.

"I could put my office in Amsterdam, and it would still be too close."

"Mmmm." His mouth makes a line from my ear to the square neckline of my dress. "You've been vice president for two weeks and I think I want to call in some of my collateral from getting you this position."

I laugh. "What shall it be this time?"

He works my skirt up over my knees. "Let's start with you naked on this rug."

"I have a meeting with finance in fifteen minutes." I giggle as he pulls down my panties.

"Then I guess I have fifteen minutes."

Rhett is nothing but prompt. Fourteen minutes and one silenced climax later, he lifts me to standing and fluffs out the smashed side of my hair. "Perfect." He assesses the rug. "It could probably stand to be about six more inches away from the sofa. I kept bumping it with my elbow."

I shove him toward the door, laughing. "Get out of here, you brute."

He turns for one final kiss before twisting the lock. But before he opens the door, he turns back to me. "I love you, Bailey Johansson."

"Oh!" He's never said this before.

He grins. "It took me a while to get the words out. I've felt it a long time."

"As long as I have?"

He draws me to him. "And how long is that?"

"Somewhere between 'Nice to meet you, Mr. Armstrong' and 'Is this my desk?'"

His smile is enormous. "Mine might have been the first time you pulled out that pink lip gloss."

"You know I can completely control you with that one little tube."

"And I love it."

We allow ourselves one more long, lingering kiss before he heads out.

I pick up the folder he left on the sofa, barely opening it before Viola pops her head in. "Bailey? I'm going to sit in on this one if that's all right with you. Jamison wanted a point person in marketing to be up to speed since you'll be at the conference next week."

Viola looks about the same, bright pink skirt, canary-yellow top, and those Jimmy Choo mules. But she's better. Since the week of meetings when Rhett and I first came back from Colorado and sat down with everyone involved in the snafu—other than Blake, who never came back—she's calmed down. She's been heard. And she really had been trying to show that Marney wasn't doing her job, leaving Viola in charge of things she couldn't always handle, while trying not to implicate me.

She's on probation for improper conduct with other employees, but everyone is watching. Rhett and I know that we're the worst out of all of us, and there's no telling what it will be like if we ever split. Dating someone in your company is a huge risk, and it never seems to end well. Viola understands the terms of staying.

So do Rhett and I.

Jamison arrives next, and as we sit on the sofa and

chairs surrounding the new rug, I try to focus on the meeting and not what just took place on it.

I'm happy here, for now, but I have plans. Big ones.

Dougherty is a stepping stone, and I'm being as up front about it as I can with Rhett, while working hard to make an impact and garner experience that will help me. I've applied to grad school, and everything I've learned will take me into the next step of my life, wiser and more confident.

When they're gone, my assistant Kate comes in. She's only been with me for a week, and is still very nervous. "Bailey? I typed up the projection sheets like you asked. I wasn't sure about some of the figures." She passes me a folder. "The digital version is in the shared folder, but I know you like numbers on paper."

"Thank you, Kate. You're doing fine. If I see some discrepancies, I'll bring you in and help you spot them. I don't expect anyone to do it perfectly when it's all so new."

She smiles. "Thank you. Will you have lunch with Mr. Armstrong here or in his office?"

I don't quite stop myself from glancing at the rug. "Have him come here. And can you order us some Thai? Our preferences are in the miscellaneous folder."

"Will do."

When she's gone, I sit at my desk, turning to survey the rug. Rhett's right. It could be farther from the sofa.

I open my notes app to jot some ideas from the meeting with finance, then take a moment to savor the space. The rug was the last piece, a joke made into reality.

Maybe Rhett did get a company from his uncle, and maybe this promotion did come about because Rhett and I are so close.

But those things don't diminish the work we've done, the plans we have, and the commitment we've shown.

I can't change where I'm from any more than Rhett can.

But we can definitely work with what we've got.

I spin back to my computer.

And that means crunching all this data before lunch, so I can bang my boyfriend in my new office.

Again.

EPILOGUE: BAILEY

One year later

Rhett appears at my office door in yellow board shorts and a bright green shirt that reads, "I'm feeling picklish."

He frowns at my wine-colored wrap dress. "Hey! Your farewell party is an island theme. What's with the fancy clothes?"

I walk around my desk, piled high with packed boxes. "They're so I could do this." I grasp the tie of the dress and strip it away. Beneath I have on a silky version of a grass hula skirt and a coconut bra.

"Now THAT'S more like it." He reaches forward with both hands as if he's going to take my coconuts.

"Bailey, you—" My assistant Kate stops in her tracks. She whirls around, and not for the first time in the last year. "Oh! Okay. You two are being you again. I'm letting you know it's time for the party." She takes off for the door.

Oh, dang. I lost track of time. That's probably why Rhett's here, too.

Rhett takes the dress and lays it over the pile of boxes on the fur rug, which he'll be moving to his office. We can't give up our favorite spot. "I'm here to escort the guest of honor."

He holds out his elbow. "Are you ready, madame vice president?"

"Ex vice president," I remind him.

"Not for another two hours. We're going to be much worse off without you."

I slide my arm through the crook of his elbow. "Martin is going to be great. I picked him myself."

"He's going to be considerably less interesting on that rug."

"Thank goodness!" Kate calls from outside the office.

Rhett and I grin at each other like teenagers busted behind the Texaco.

By the time we walk into the meeting room, everyone is assembled.

"Wow!" I call. "This is amazing!"

And it is. A makeshift hut with a straw roof like the one on the island has been assembled on the side wall. The counter is filled with a taco bar and mocktails. Peter from maintenance is serving as the bartender, even though his daiquiris are virgin and the piña colada is all juice and coconut.

He holds up an enormous glass goblet. "What's your poison?"

I look over the food. "With tacos, I'd say strawberry daiquiri!"

"You got it." He drops strawberries into a blender with a scoop of ice, then pours in simple syrup.

I turn to look over the crowd. I swear I recognize some of the getups from a year ago. Marney in marketing, whose role was downgraded since she wasn't able to keep up with her former workload, is wearing the same striped sundress with her orthopedics that I remember from the cruise.

Viola has her white mesh back, only this time it's covering hot pink skater shorts and a black sports bra.

The crew is colorful, that's for sure. It's a lovely, bright send-off.

"And here you are, milady," Peter says, handing me the oversized glass. I notice everyone else has plastic cups. When I look more closely at it, I see the words, "Bailey Johansson, VP of Marketing, Island Survivor."

"I love it," I tell him. "Thank you."

Caribbean music creates a melodic undertone beneath the hum of conversation. Rhett grabs a drink, and we walk among the staff, accepting handshakes and hugs.

I'm going to miss this place.

Gloria wanders up. "When do classes start?"

"Two weeks. I'm still trying to switch one credit."

"A masters in poly sci," Gloria says. "It's a brave choice."

"Depends on what I do with it," I say.

Rhett leans in. "She'll use her power for good."

"I'm sure she will." Gloria squeezes my arm. "Martin seems great, but we will miss you around here."

"I'll miss you all, too."

The music grows louder, and everyone realizes at once that it's a conga line song.

"Hi yi yi yi!" Hammond from IT calls out, his neck encircled with plastic leis. He starts rolling his hands to the beat, and others fall in behind. They form a long snake in the center of the room, pulling up anyone seated on the chairs along the wall.

Rhett takes my drink from me right as I'm swept into the fray.

We conga through the meeting room, down the hall, to the elevator, and back. When we return, the music has switched to something else entirely, and everyone breaks apart with laughter.

"We out conga'd the conga!" Hammond shouts.

Rhett returns my glass to me. He's holding a tray of oysters.

"Oh, not again," I say. I haven't touched them since we were stranded on the island.

"Try the one in the middle," Rhett says. "It's special."

I hold up my hand. "Oh no, nobody's going to make me slurp raw sea creatures."

Gloria returns, her eyes oddly glittery. "Just take a peek inside."

I realize everyone is looking at me, and the music has been turned down.

"What is this?" I ask.

Rhett waits, his eyes imploring me to do as he asks.

I think I know what's happening.

I lift the center oyster from the tray. Rhett's gaze follows my movements, and when I look up, I sense the intensity of the moment.

Gloria takes the tray as I hold the one he directed me to choose. These oysters have both shells, so I lift the top.

Inside the clean, shining shell is a diamond ring, a perfect oval surrounded by bright, clear gems. It's enormous.

I glance up at Rhett's face, but it isn't there.

He's dropped to one knee.

He reaches up to pluck the ring from the polished shell and takes my free hand. "Bailey, we've worked together for three years, but in all that time, we never surpassed the partnership we formed on the island when left all alone and forced to form an alliance to survive."

He looks up at me, his dark hair falling across his forehead, the close-clipped beard he's kept lately reminding me of how he looked after a couple of days on the island.

With the hut in my peripheral vision, and all the staff decked out in their vacation duds, I feel almost transported to the cruise.

"Bailey, this last year has been nothing short of magical. With you by my side, I've grown not only as someone in charge of a thriving company, but also as a man who needed to find his way.

"And I have found it. With you. So will you please make me the happiest man alive and be my wife?"

I swear I can hear the roar of the ocean and smell

the salty air. I'm not sure how two people could go so far in how they feel about each other from then to now.

But I do know that I love him.

And I've known for a long time how he feels about me.

"Yes," I tell him. "Yes, Rhett Michael Armstrong, I will marry you."

His smile is huge as he slides the ring on my finger, then we realize it's the wrong hand, and I move the oyster's shell to the other hand and we switch the ring.

Everyone laughs and sends up a great huzzah and clinks their glasses. My daiquiri is returned, and this time I smell rum. Someone's spiked it! Peter gives me a big thumbs up as Rhett and I intertwine our arms like brides and grooms do on their wedding day.

And we take a good, long drink to our future.

Thank you for reading Juicy Pickle! You're knee-deep in the Pickleverse, so don't stop now!

Pickles mentioned in this book who have love stories of their own:

- **Rhett's brother Axel** meets his match on a hiking trail in a situation only a rom com could get away with in Tasty Pickle.
- Want to learn how **Havannah's castle** came about? Read about how she goes into labor on her first date with billionaire Donvan in Tasty Mango.

- **Uncle Sherman** raised a whole brood of sons. Read their hilarious adventures in romance in the original Pickle trilogy: Big Pickle, Hot Pickle, and Spicy Pickle.

BOOKS BY JJ KNIGHT

Romantic Comedies

Single Dad on Top

The Accidental Harem

Big Pickle ~ Hot Pickle ~ Spicy Pickle

Royal Pickle ~ Royal Rebel ~ Royal Escape

Tasty Mango ~ Tasty Pickle

Juicy Pickle

The Wedding Confession

The Wedding Shake-up

Second Chance Santa

MMA Fighters

Uncaged Love

Fight for Her

Reckless Attraction

Get emails or texts from JJ about her new releases at www.
jjknight.com/news

ABOUT JJ KNIGHT

JJ Knight is one of the pen names of six-time *USA Today* bestselling author Deanna Roy. She lives in Austin, Texas, with her family.

To choose your next read from one of her fifty books, visit the web site **ReadLaughSwoon.com** to pick by book boyfriend, story line, heat level and more!

facebook.com/jjknightauthor

x.com/deannaroy

instagram.com/deannaroyauthor

bookbub.com/profile/jj-knight

tiktok.com/@jjknight.author